DANGEROUS PROTECTOR

RED STONE SECURITY SERIES

Katie Reus

Cover art: Jaycee of Sweet 'N Spicy Designs
Editors: JRT Editing & AKA Editorial Services
Author website: http://www.katiereus.com

Publisher's Note: This is a work of fiction. Names, characters, places, and incidents are either the products of the author's imagination or used fictitiously, and any resemblance to actual persons, living or dead, or business establishments, organizations or locales is completely coincidental.

Dangerous Protector/Katie Reus. -- 1st ed.

ISBN-10: 1942447523
ISBN-13: 9781942447528

eISBN: 9781942447511

For my husband.

Praise for the novels of Katie Reus

"Sexy military romantic suspense!" —USA Today

"...a wild hot ride for readers. The story grabs you and doesn't let go."
—*New York Times* bestselling author, Cynthia Eden

"Has all the right ingredients: a hot couple, evil villains, and a killer
action-filled plot. . . . [The] Moon Shifter series is what I call Grade-
A entertainment!" —Joyfully Reviewed

"I could not put this book down. . . . Let me be clear that I am not
saying that this was a good book *for* a paranormal genre; it was an
excellent romance read, *period.*" —All About Romance

"Reus strikes just the right balance of steamy sexual tension and nail-
biting action....This romantic thriller reliably hits every note that
fans of the genre will expect." —*Publishers Weekly*

"Prepare yourself for the start of a great new series! . . . I'm excited
about reading more about this great group of characters."
—Fresh Fiction

"Wow! This powerful, passionate hero sizzles with sheer
deliciousness. I loved every sexy twist of this fun & exhilarating tale.
Katie Reus delivers!" —Carolyn Crane, RITA award winning author

Continued...

CHAPTER ONE

Tegan didn't turn around at the sound of the little bell jingling over the front door. She knew exactly who was coming into Kimmy's Cakes and Coffee at seven thirty in the morning. Callan Fitzpatrick. Recent military vet, quiet and sweet, he'd been coming in here every morning for the past month to flirt with Tegan's boss, Kimmy.

Well, sort of flirt. The two of them were hopeless—and adorable—as they danced around each other. She hoped Callan worked up the courage to ask her friend out.

"I'll have your order in just a sec. Kimmy's coming in later—Brendan's got a fever. So you're stuck looking at me this morning."

"That's not exactly a hardship." A deep, familiar, and oh-so-sexy male voice made everything inside her go still. *Not* Callan, but his older brother, Aaron. The man affected her in ways she didn't even want to think about.

Especially since most of the time he didn't seem to even like her.

Pasting on her most pleasant expression, she turned from the espresso coffee grinder. Like always, she felt a jolt of awareness when she saw him. Something—everything—about him called to her on a level she didn't quite understand. Tall, dark, and perpetually surly. Except when he had his five-year-old son with him. *Then* he was actually human. Unfortunately for her, Aaron was alone today so that meant she got the surly version. Though, so far he actually seemed to be in a decent mood.

"That almost sounded like a compliment." Smiling, the action more nervous than anything, she reached for the stack of to-go cups.

He lifted one of those big shoulders. "Just the truth."

She so did *not* know what to make of that. "Same order as always?"

"Yep." He shoved his hands in his jacket pockets and looked around the shop curiously, as if he cared about the feminine French-style decorations.

Kimmy was obsessed with fleurs-de-lis and they were everywhere. Even the miniature chandelier, which was more for decoration than actual use, had little dangling fleurs-de-lis that glittered when the sun hit the shop just right. Since it was almost Christmas, there were a few extra decorations, including a small tree in one corner with red and white little fleurs-de-lis ornaments Kimmy had made herself with a lot of glitter, paint, and ribbon. Tegan tried to ignore the fact that she'd be alone again this Christmas, but seeing it splashed everywhere, even at work, made it difficult.

Aaron didn't come in here very often, but Tegan still figured his intent observation of the place was to avoid looking at or talking to her. Which made something perverse in her flare to life. She wasn't sure what it was, but his refusal to look at her made her want to *make* him talk to her.

"Coming right up," she said as she moved to the economy-sized coffeemaker. She'd already ground the beans this morning. And unlike the majority of customers who wanted a specialty drink, both Fitzpatrick brothers drank their coffees black with sugar. This would be her easiest order of the day. "Feel like mixing it up this morning?" With her back to him, she glanced up in the mirror over the prep station.

He was looking at her back with a mix of emotions. Annoyance and...hunger? She blinked. That couldn't be right. Well, the annoyance was probably spot on, even if she didn't know what she'd done to bother him. Maybe he just didn't like redheads. Which was ridiculous, since gingers were awesome.

"How so?" he rumbled in that deep voice that flowed right through her like hot chocolate on a winter day, warming her from the inside out.

She ignored what the sound of it did to her insides. "Go wild, get some cannolis for the guys at work. They would be eternally grateful, trust me." She knew he worked for the same security company her friend Julieta's husband did, though she wasn't precisely sure what he did. Just something to do with personal security.

He made a grunting sound of derision. "No, thanks."

"Fine, but you're taking a few chocolate macarons to give to Dillon. They're on me." Because she adored Aaron's son. The kid was always so serious when he came into the shop and she enjoyed making him smile. Usually Tegan's dog, Kali, did that job with no problem when she was here. It was hard for anyone not to smile when a sweet Siberian husky was giving you kisses and wagging her tail like you were the most important person in the world to her.

His entire body—muscular, trim, and fit—went still. "How do you know he likes those?"

She lifted an eyebrow. "Uh, because I work here and he comes in two days a week with your mom."

He blinked, as if this news surprised him. Uh-oh, maybe it was a grandma-grandson secret since Bree Fitzpatrick *did* let Dillon get whatever he wanted. Like, always. She literally never said no to the kid when he asked for something. Tegan was about to backtrack when he nodded. "Yeah, bag some up."

"Want to get some lemon ones for Bree? She loves them." She held back a grin, wondering if she was pushing him too much.

Those brown eyes that weren't just a plain, boring brown but had amber flecks in them watched her with curiosity. "I can see why Kimmy hired you. You're very good at upselling." Again, she wasn't sure if that was a compliment or not. His tone and facial expressions were impossible to read. Frustrating man.

"Well, yeah, I'm awesome." Now she smiled at him, unable not to.

His lips twitched a fraction, and she couldn't help but wonder what he would look like if he actually gave her a full-on smile. He'd no doubt be knee-weakening gorgeous so it was probably a good thing he was allergic to smiling. "Yeah, throw some of those in, too."

She bagged the sweet macarons into the small pink and white bags. They carried simple brown bags that Kimmy usually gave to male customers, but Aaron was getting the pink. The thought of such a huge, sexy guy carrying these around made her smile. "Sure you don't want some extras to surprise your coworkers?"

He just snorted, which was apparently his version of no.

God, what was wrong with her? She needed to just shut up but she couldn't turn off her mouth or her brain around him. "The lemon ones are melt-in-your-mouth zesty and delicious."

At that, his gaze dipped to *her* mouth, paused, and for just a fraction of a second lust flared in his gaze so bright and hot she felt the burn straight to her toes. Oh, sweet Lord. Then he did that typical Aaron thing and just grunted a nonresponse, slid cash on the counter, and left with his coffee.

She watched his very tight backside as he stalked from the shop. And stalked was the only word for the way he was moving. His back was rigid, his shoulders tight.

She seriously wished she could figure him out. At twenty-seven, Tegan had been on the receiving end of more than her share of appreciative male looks and Aaron had definitely given off that vibe—for less than a second.

Or maybe she was just projecting because something about Aaron Fitzpatrick got to her. Got under her skin in the worst way possible. Before she'd settled down in Miami eight months ago she'd been on the run for two solid years. Sex hadn't been on her agenda. The opposite sex in general had barely registered to her because all she'd cared about was staying one step ahead of the man hunting her. Now that her threat was dead, she had time to actually live again.

So why did her libido have to wake up and take notice of the grumpiest man she'd ever met? When she saw he'd left one of the macaron bags behind, she snapped it up.

After locking the cash register, she stepped out from behind the counter. Normally she wouldn't leave the shop unattended, but they wouldn't get busy for another twenty minutes. While crime wasn't completely nonexistent, it was on the low side on this particular street and in this part of town. It was one of the reasons she'd decided to work here. She wanted way less stress in her life after the last couple of years.

Aaron was across the street, arms folded over his chest as he leaned against his parked truck while he talked to Addie, the owner of a painting shop. She ran Addie's Bring Your Own Brush and had 'paint parties' five or six days a week.

He must have set the coffee inside his vehicle. Neither of them had seen her so it gave her a chance to watch him when he was unguarded. His expression was relaxed, his body language loose and casual. Tegan moved between two vehicles parked by the curb and waited for a car to drive past before she stepped into the road.

It shouldn't bother her so much, or at all really, but he was so relaxed talking to Addie. It was as if he just saved his grumpiness for Tegan. She bit back the sigh that wanted to escape. It didn't matter. As she crossed the road, both Aaron and Addie looked up. Since she was friendly with Addie, Tegan smiled. "Hey, I like what you've done with your hair."

"Thanks." She fingered the newly chopped off locks. Addie had worn her thick brown hair past her shoulders for as long as Tegan had known her, which admittedly wasn't that long. Now it shaped around her face in a sleek bob that showed off her elegant features. "I needed a change."

Addie and her long-time boyfriend had recently broken up, and good riddance to the guy as far as Tegan was concerned. She'd only met him twice and the guy had that skeezy vibe all over him. All fake charm that Tegan knew was just a veneer. After being on the run she'd learned to read people fast. "Well, you look great. Blake can eat his heart out when he sees you."

Addie laughed, shaking her head. "I hope so."

"You forgot these." Tegan handed the bag to Aaron, avoiding his gaze and ignoring the little spark that flared when their fingers brushed.

"How's your painting coming along?" Addie asked when Tegan would have made her quick getaway.

She glanced over her shoulder. There were two joggers heading down the opposite sidewalk. Unlikely they'd head into Kimmy's shop, but she needed to be there in case they did. "Ah..." She turned back to Addie and winced. "Awful, to be honest. Spectacularly awful. I don't think I have that creative gene."

"I don't believe that. I've gotten so many compliments on that website redesign you did. But come to the next class this Thursday afternoon if you're free. I'll figure out where you're struggling. We'll fix it, I promise."

The truth was Tegan would rather just *buy* a cute painting, but it would be pretty cool to actually finish one herself. *Once.* Because after she finished this thing, she was done with painting. And it was unlikely she'd be hanging it where anyone could see it either. Maybe in her closet. "I'll be there. I'll bring some treats, too."

Addie's blue eyes lit up. "Bring those chocolate chip cannolis."

"I will, but I've gotta get back to the shop." She glanced over her shoulder again just in time to see Mrs. Bailey strolling down the sidewalk, bundled up in a scarf, hat, thick jacket, and walking her little shih tzu—who had on a tiny pink hat and matching doggy coat. She opened the door to Kimmy's shop and stepped inside. Duty called.

As she started to jog back across the street, a chilly breeze whipped over her. She hadn't bothered to grab her jacket, but now she wished she had. Wearing jeans, a long-sleeved black T-shirt, and a black-and-white checkered apron wasn't helping much with the chill.

When she reached the sidewalk she stuck her hand in the pocket of her apron. She'd get too warm wearing her jacket inside, but she could use an extra sweater today. She'd just grab the one she'd left in her car. It was a surprisingly cold winter in Florida. She was counting down the days until spring.

Her car was a few shops down as she pressed the key fob to unlock the doors. The moment she did, an explosion of noise and heat ripped through the air. Glass seemed to rain down from everywhere, pinging against cars, the sidewalk, and scraping her neck.

Screaming, Tegan threw herself to the sidewalk, covering her head as she dove. Another scream built in her throat, but it was too tight to escape as another shockwave of energy seemed to roll over her, pulsing through her entire body.

As she rolled for the curb, her stomach slammed into a light pole. Grunting in pain, she tried to push away from it, but couldn't make herself move. Her head throbbed and all the muscles in her body were pulled tight.

Full-blown terror rocked through her as it belatedly registered that had been *her* car that had just exploded.

If she'd been closer to it or *inside* it...

Oh God, she'd parked right outside the children's clothing boutique. If that thing had gone off a couple of hours later...

Tremors overtook her body, making her shake so badly she couldn't move, could barely think. The man who'd wanted something from her that she simply didn't have, had been killed. He *couldn't* be after her.

But someone obviously wanted her dead. You didn't accidentally rig a bomb in someone's car.

When a strong hand took her by the shoulder, she moved on pure instinct and struck out, letting years' worth of raw survival instinct explode as her fist connected with hard flesh.

CHAPTER TWO

Aaron caught her fist in his open palm. "Tegan! It's me!"

All the energy left Tegan's body in a whoosh. It was Aaron, not someone who had come back from the grave to finish her off. Her heart still beat an erratic tattoo against her chest, but her fight instinct was quickly fading.

Aaron bent over her, his far too handsome face a mask of concern. "Tegan, can you hear me?"

Nausea swept through her as she stared up into the most beautiful dark, amber-flecked eyes she'd ever seen. In the distance she was vaguely aware of multiple car alarms going off and the sounds of worried shouts. Probably from shop owners or early morning joggers. At least most of the shops weren't open this early.

"Damn it, Tegan, answer me." He looked away from her then and she heard him shout out orders to someone to call 911. It sounded as if he was in a tunnel as he spoke.

He held up three fingers in front of her. "How many fingers am I holding up? What day is it?"

The ringing in her ears suddenly stopped, as if a switch had been flipped. Groaning, she swatted at his hand. "Three, and Tuesday, I think."

The relief that crossed his face was so stark she felt it like a physical caress. "There was an explosion and you were close. You need to stay still. The shockwaves from an explosion can travel through the body at a rapid speed—including through the brain. It can actually move the brain in the skull. You need to stay where you are." He spoke so clinically, but the note of worry in his voice was impossible to ignore.

"Jeez, Aaron. That's so gross. Are you trying to freak me out more?" Why on earth would he tell her all this? She shoved his hands away and sat up. Pricks of pain stabbed her palms as she pushed against the sidewalk. Wincing, she saw the blanket of glass shards littering the sidewalk around them.

Cursing under his breath, he gently took one of her palms and started pulling the fragments from her skin. "Your car just exploded in a fiery ball. I think that should freak you out more than anything. You could have a concussion, and we need to keep you still until help gets here." Sharp fear punctuated each word. "Not that I like just being a sitting duck," he muttered, looking around and waving off anyone who tried to get too close to her.

"Your bedside manner sucks." She tried not to flinch as he pulled out the glass pieces.

Maybe it was the mention of the word *bed* but his dark gaze flicked to hers and momentarily did that heated thing again before he returned to his task. Or more likely it was just her imagination.

"How do you know that stuff about concussions and explosions anyway?"

He paused and glanced up at the sound of an approaching ambulance. Oh, thank God, help was on the way. "I was in the Corps."

Oh right, she knew that. "I thought the Marines had corpsmen from the Navy as their medical people." She knew she was rambling but didn't care. She was feeling shaky and needed to talk.

"How do you know that?" Job complete, he let go of her hand. Was it just her imagination or did he linger a moment before letting go?

"My dad was in the Navy." Grimacing, she twisted back and forth to see if she had full range of movement. Nothing seemed to be broken. Of course, now she was freaked out about what he'd said. She kept envisioning her brain moving around in her skull like Jell-O, which didn't help her nausea.

"Tell me about your dad." His voice was utterly calm as he held up a hand to a concerned-looking jogger about twenty feet away, ordering the guy to move back in a ridiculously authoritative voice.

She was grateful he was keeping people at bay. He seemed almost vigilant about it, not letting anyone near—probably because he was worried that whoever had set that bomb might be around. Oh God. She didn't even want to think about that right now. She cleared her throat. "Why?"

"Just talk to me. I don't know anything about your past and I'm curious."

"You've never been curious before."

"I need to keep you talking in case you *do* have a concussion."

The sirens were growing louder now. "I should have tried getting blown up months ago if that's what it takes to get you to be nice to me."

"I'm nice." He actually sounded offended.

She snorted then winced at the rush of pain that shuddered through the base of her skull. "Holy balls, my head hurts."

"God, your mouth." The way he said it almost sounded like a groan.

"I think you like my mouth." The instant the words were out she wished she could reel them back in. Oh yeah, *clearly* she had a concussion. Or freaking brain damage.

To her surprise, his lips pulled up in the first honest to God smile she'd ever seen from him. It completely transformed his constantly gruff expression into something that should be considered illegal. "You wouldn't be wrong about that," he murmured.

Wait...what? She swore her heart actually stuttered in her chest. Before she could even think of a half-decent response, he stood from his crouching position and started shouting at someone. Tegan wanted to cover her ears.

Seconds later two uniformed paramedics hustled Aaron out of the way. She wanted to ask him to stay, but knew that was stupid. They weren't friends and even though he made her feel safe, she wasn't going to put herself out there like that. Crouching in front of her, a female paramedic introduced herself and started taking Tegan's vitals, all while asking her rapid-fire questions.

While Tegan answered, the two paramedics helped her onto a stretcher.

She was finally able to take in the complete, horrific landscape. On her side of the street, the windows of Addie's shop, a hardware store, and the children's boutique clothing store had all been blown out. Tegan's car was a smoldering mass of metal, shattered glass, and twisted plastic. The vehicles in front and behind it had also been affected by the blast, all the glass blown out and now littering the sidewalk and street. It looked like a war zone.

One of her side-view mirrors lay on the sidewalk, flames flickering along the rounded top of it. Bystanders had been partitioned off across the street as the police worked to create a barricade around the blast site.

Panic punched out to all her nerve endings. "Oh God, is anyone else hurt?"

"Just you that we know about." The blond woman with tattoos peeking out at her wrist moved efficiently as she got Tegan settled into place.

Beyond exhausted, she closed her eyes and lay back against the stretcher. She didn't want to see anyone right now, not even her friends.

"Don't go to sleep on me," Blondie snapped as they started moving her.

"I'm not. I just don't want to see anyone."

"Fair enough until we get you in the ambulance."

Tegan just wanted to curl into a ball and hide. Had she somehow brought her past troubles to Miami? The man who'd been after her was dead. She should have been safe.

As they lifted her onto the back of the ambulance, her eyes popped open at the sound of Aaron's deep, annoyed voice.

"Damn it, be careful with her." He was glowering at the paramedics as he climbed in after them.

A ridiculous surge of elation slid through her to see him.

"Don't tell me how to do my job, Aaron." The woman's mouth pulled into a thin line and Tegan realized how much they looked alike.

She knew the Fitzpatrick brothers didn't have any other siblings so maybe the woman was a cousin. "Are you coming with me?" she asked him.

Aaron seemed truly surprised by her question. "You thought I was just going to let you go to the hospital alone?"

Well, yeah, she had. "Oh God! The shop—"

"Don't worry about it. I already called Kimmy, and Addie is locking up until she can get down here. She's got an extra key."

Another thought slammed into her and the panic she'd been keeping at bay started to bloom out of control. "My dog—"

"Took care of that, too. Addie said you'd be worried. She's calling your neighbor to let her know what's going on."

"Thank you. I..." Tegan trailed off as Blondie told him to shut up and stay out of the way before she kicked him off the ambulance.

Tegan was grateful for his solid presence and was thankful when he obeyed the woman because she didn't want him kicked off. He grew quiet and moved to the only free seat, right in Tegan's line of sight. Seeing him there gave her strength she knew she was going to need.

Soon enough, she knew the police or a detective would be at the hospital to question her. Which meant all her past secrets were about to come spilling out. Just great. Aaron already seemed to judge her or dislike her for whatever reason—today's behavior was an anomaly. He definitely wouldn't like her once he heard all about her past.

* * *

Arms crossed over his chest, Aaron stood next to Tegan's hospital bed as the doctor spoke quietly to her. She hadn't lost consciousness during the explosion so that was a good sign. He'd been worried she had internal injuries but the doctor had more or less determined that she had a very mild concussion. Which wasn't great, but considering the alternative, he was grateful how minor her injuries were. Other than that and the few scrapes on her palms, she was okay. Just shaken up. Not that he could blame her.

When his gaze strayed to her pale face, his gut tightened. She'd pulled her dark auburn hair up into a ponytail since arriving at the hospital, but a few strands had come loose, framing her bright blue eyes and sharp cheekbones. Freckles dotted across her nose and cheeks, making her look younger than he knew her to be.

He still couldn't get the image of that explosion out of his head. Even when he closed his eyes. She could have been in that car. He scrubbed a hand over his face, wishing he could banish the horror that wanted to keep replaying in his head, over and over.

He'd seen his share of death and it wasn't pretty. Some movies liked to romanticize war, but during his four tours in Afghanistan and Iraq he knew there was nothing glamorous about it, especially death. The sight and stench of burning bodies was something no one should have to experience.

"Mr. Fitzpatrick."

His eyes snapped open at the doctor's voice. "Yes?"

Dr. Morales nodded once at him. "I want to keep Miss O'Kelly here for another hour of observation. There's a detective waiting to talk to her anyway so she might be here longer than that. I need to know if you'll be able to drive her home—"

"That's not necessary. I can call someone to get me." Tegan's brow furrowed and Aaron had the most ridiculous urge to smooth out the lines.

Whenever he was around her, he simply wanted to touch her, to see if her ivory skin was as soft as it looked. Nothing would ever come of his fantasies, but that didn't seem to stop them. She was a combination of sassy and sensual. At maybe five foot two, she was petite and curvy with a bottom lip that always seemed to be pouty. He'd had way too many thoughts over the last eight months about what it would be like to take that lip between his teeth, to stroke his tongue between her lips...

Hell, he needed to focus. Tegan wasn't for him. "I'll take you, Tegan. Let me do it. Please." Because he didn't want to leave her side. He wasn't sure what that was about either, but when he'd seen her fly back after that explosion, out of his line of vision when she tumbled behind that car, he'd lost years of his life as he raced to her. Right now he was feeling protective. Probably irrationally so. But he needed to make sure she was okay.

"Only because you said please," she murmured, a smile ghosting her face.

God, he loved her smile.

"I've written her a prescription for a strong nonsteroidal anti-inflammatory drug. But Tylenol or Advil will work, too. If she wants the prescription, you'll need to pick it up before taking her home. Make sure she takes it." The doctor glanced over at Tegan. "You can't take anything with codeine or any sort of opiate in it. I don't know that it's necessary given the mildness of your concussion, but it wouldn't hurt to have someone wake you up every few hours tonight. We want to make sure you're not too sluggish."

Before she could respond, Aaron cut in. "I'll take care of her."

Out of the corner of his eye, he could see she wanted to protest, but instead crossed her arms over her chest and settled back against the bed. She'd protested putting on the hospital gown, but had done it anyway. Now it gaped at her neckline, showing off all sorts of smooth, kissable skin. He felt like a bastard for even noticing.

"Good. I—"

A sharp knock sounded on the door, then it opened. Detective Carlito Duarte—a man Aaron had called in as a favor—stepped into the room, his expression grim.

"You need more time?" he asked the doctor after a nod at Aaron.

"We're done here." He turned back to Tegan, his expression softening. "I'm going to write that prescription but if you need anything, buzz the nurses. You were very lucky."

She nodded and for the first time since everything had happened, tears filled her eyes. "I will, and thanks."

As the doctor left, Carlito stepped farther into the room. "How're you feeling, Miss O'Kelly?"

"Good as can be expected. And just call me Tegan."

"Okay...I need to ask you some questions," he said, looking at Aaron now, his intent clear. He wanted Aaron to clear out.

Aaron took another step closer to her bed so that he was right next to her head. He wasn't going anywhere unless Tegan asked him to. "I'm not leaving—I was a witness, too."

"Can he stay, please?" Tegan's quiet voice pulled both their attention to her.

Carlito nodded, though his expression was annoyed. Aaron didn't care. He wasn't leaving Tegan.

Aaron was a little surprised she'd asked, but thankful. He figured she'd need some support and he wanted to be it. He knew what it was like to be laid up in a hospital room, alone with no one there when he woke up. Not even remotely the same circumstances, but he simply couldn't leave her now. As far as he knew she didn't have any family here. Or any family at all, really. He'd asked his brother, who was friendly with her, and Callan had seemed to think she was alone.

Aaron had already called work to let them know he wouldn't be in today and he'd asked his brother to pick Dillon up from school so there was nothing dragging him away from her bedside.

"He can stay as long as you want him here." Carlito's voice dropped to a softer, speaking-to-a-victim tone, and for that Aaron was grateful.

When he pulled up a chair on Tegan's other side, Aaron did the same with a rolling stool and sat next to her. He had the most irrational urge to take her hand in his, but resisted.

"As you can imagine, I've got some questions for you. I've already spoken to some of the eyewitnesses, but I need to confirm that your vehicle was the one that exploded." Carlito rattled off a license plate number and held out a digital camera. The screen showed a picture of her mottled, ruined car, pieces of it strewn across the street and sidewalk.

She wrapped her arms around herself as she nodded. "Yeah, that's it. It exploded when I pressed my key fob to unlock it. I'd come outside to give Aaron part of his order he forgot, and on my way back to the shop I decided to grab my sweater since a jacket would be too heavy. And...I'm rambling. Yes, that's my car."

"You're not rambling. I want as many details as you can remember. Is it normal for you to go to your car during the day?"

"No. I almost never leave the shop when I'm working. But we don't get our rush until about eight, so..." Her face grew even paler. "I was supposed to leave around noon today during the shift change. That's one of the busiest times downtown." Tegan started to breathe harder, wheezing in and out in a panic, so Aaron slid a hand behind her back and started rubbing up and down in a soothing motion.

Her gown only tied at the neck so all he felt was smooth, soft skin. No bra, something he didn't want to be noticing.

"Do you want a glass of water?" Carlito asked as she started to get herself back under control.

Aaron still didn't remove his hand and she didn't seem to want him to. Touching her was stupid for his sanity, but he didn't care. She needed comfort right now.

"No, I'm good. I want to help you find who did this."

"I'm going to start with the obvious. Do you know of anyone who could have wanted to harm you? Any enemies, ex-boyfriends? From what I heard from some of the eyewitnesses, you've done a lot of design work for the shops downtown, so what about other freelance work? It's a stretch, but any contracts that didn't work out? I want the names of absolutely anyone you can think of."

Chewing on her bottom lip, she flicked a wary glance at Aaron before she looked back at the detective. "There's only one person I can think of who would want to hurt me enough to kill me, but he's dead."

Aaron almost jolted at that, but remained where he was, his palm on her back. Her heartbeat had evened out now. What the hell? The thought of anyone trying to hurt her made all his protective instincts rise up.

Her gaze dropped to her lap. "Have you ever heard of a man named Enzo De Fiore?"

It sounded vaguely familiar to Aaron, but he couldn't place it. Duarte seemed to be having the same issue. "That sounds familiar."

"He is—was—a gangster in Chicago. Before he died eight months ago, he was convinced that I helped my brother steal a bunch of diamonds from him. Diamonds that *he* already stole from someone else. I didn't take them, but that didn't matter to him. Before I settled here I was on the run for two solid years because he was convinced I knew something." Her cheeks flushed a delicate shade of pink. He couldn't be sure, but she looked almost guilty as she continued.

"I didn't take his diamonds, but...I did steal his dog when I ran."

CHAPTER THREE

Enzo slammed his fist against the steering wheel but it didn't make him feel any better. Nothing would make him better until he got his fucking diamonds. He'd been watching that little bitch Tegan for a few weeks now and her lifestyle wasn't like someone who had a stash of millions of dollars' worth of diamonds at her disposal.

He'd have gone after her sooner but he had other shit to worry about—like the Feds not believing he was really dead. Coming after Tegan and potentially showing his face in Miami eight months ago would have been stupid. Especially with all the CCTVs they had in the city. So he'd done what he had to do. He'd lain low in a back-woods small town in the middle of nowhere until the time was right. He hadn't been in the news lately so he'd sent his partner ahead to get a place ready for him, a place close to Tegan.

Ever since, he'd been watching and waiting for the right opportunity to make a move.

Then she'd almost gotten herself killed in town today. So now he was sitting in the hospital parking lot while she was inside hopefully not fucking dead.

He wasn't sure who would want to kill her—other than him, of course. Maybe she'd double-crossed a partner when she'd taken his damn diamonds. And deep down he knew she had to have had a partner. Probably her brother. Though that fucker was a ghost, long gone. Enzo hadn't even gotten a hint of where he might be. He didn't think her brother would try to blow her up though...no, there had to be someone else involved with her. Or maybe she'd stolen from someone else after him?

It didn't matter. Whoever wanted her dead would just have to wait.

She couldn't die until he got what he wanted—hell, *needed*. Those diamonds were his ticket out of the country, away from the federal charges he'd be facing if the FBI knew he was still alive, his key to escaping his life of crime. He was tired of always looking over his shoulder, wondering who might try to kill him from day to day. He just wanted to retire comfortably. He deserved it after all.

Keeping his ball cap tugged low, he pulled out his cell phone.

His partner answered on the first ring. "Yeah?"

"How is she?"

"Good. From what I hear, she just has a mild concussion. Maybe not even that. Cops are here, though. A detective, I think, and some guy, one of the witnesses. He apparently works for a security company, but I don't know more than that."

Now would be the perfect time to search her place. With her damn dog that she'd stolen from him, and her schedule—*and* her nosy neighbors—it had been impossible to get inside. Even now it was a risk because there was no guarantee a neighbor wouldn't see him. But if she was at the hospital he had to take this chance, since it was clear someone wanted her dead. No one was getting his diamonds. No one. "I'm going to search her place. Call me when she leaves the hospital."

"Okay."

He ended the call without responding further. There was nothing else to say anyway.

The drive to Tegan's place didn't take long even with traffic, but his heart was pounding erratically the entire time.

She could have died today. If it hadn't been for what sounded like dumb luck, she would have. Then where would he be? Fucked, that's where. The last eight months he'd been in hiding, she'd been setting up her pathetic little life. He thought he had plenty of time to go after her, time for her to get comfortable, to put roots down—to start *using* those diamonds.

Now to know that someone else wanted her dead moved his timeline up drastically. It might blow his cover and prove that he wasn't dead, but if pushed, he'd just take her and torture the information out of her. Hell, it was what he should have done back in Chicago. He'd made a mistake with her, had thought she'd be too afraid to cross him. That was one mistake he wouldn't make again.

After driving by her place twice, he parked a few blocks over and made his way to her townhome. Instead of going up to the front door, he kept walking around the side of the place. The townhomes were like little gingerbread houses, all lined up and perfect with clusters of palm trees in every yard. The majority of the people who lived here were in their twenties but there were some older, retirement age people in the neighbor-hood—including one of Tegan's neighbors.

An old woman who was always looking out her win-dow, clearly worrying what her neighbors were doing.

So he avoided her and walked briskly around the op-posite side of Tegan's place. There wasn't much space in between the residences. When he reached the end of the townhouse he peered around and saw her small back porch.

Just a round table, two chairs, and a charcoal grill in front of a sliding glass door. Looked like it always did. He hurried onto the back porch and made quick work of the door. It took longer than he'd have liked to get inside but he didn't want to break the glass and risk drawing attention to himself.

Sweat dripped down his face despite the cool weath-er as he finally got the latch free and quietly slid inside. No alarm went off. She didn't have a sign outside that she had an alarm system, but not all people did. He let out a sigh of relief when everything remained quiet. He'd been avoiding breaking in in case she had a security system, but now he'd been pushed to his limit.

He shoved the long curtain out of his way and quick-ly surveyed his surroundings. The place looked normal enough, though certainly not high end. A couch, loveseat, big-screen television, some prints on the wall. Even though it was almost Christmas she didn't have any decorations. None that he could see. Not even a tree. He stepped farther into the room, his pulse accelerating.

If he were in her shoes and wanted to hide diamonds, he'd keep them close. In his bedroom. In a safe.

Deeper into the house, he froze when an alarm beeped, the shrill sound grating against his nerves. That was when he saw the sensor in the corner of the room.

Damn it.

The sliding glass door might not have a security contact, but she still had a system in place. For a long moment he debated his options. It would take the police at least ten minutes to get there. But that old bitch next door might come over. He had no problem killing the woman but that would take time and would slow his escape. Not to mention if he stabbed her he'd end up with blood on him. He couldn't be walking around with blood spattered all over his clothes. Not if he wanted to remain invisible. Plus, he wasn't prepared for a kill today and he'd no doubt leave evidence behind if he killed someone. If his DNA got into any online database the Feds would be all over Miami looking for him. Yeah, time to get the hell out of there.

Jaw clenched, he backtracked toward the sliding glass door. He'd make a quick exit and be long gone before the cops arrived. As he passed one of the side tables, he saw a picture of Tegan smiling widely with her arm slung around a full-grown husky.

Anger surged through him at the sight. Unable to control his rage, he knocked it off the table, watching as it slammed to the ground before hurrying back the way he'd broken in.

Time to disappear. For now. But he'd be back. Next time he was going to get what he wanted.

* * *

The handsome detective and Aaron both looked at Tegan with a mix of surprise and possibly horror.

Aaron was the first to speak. "You stole a gangster's dog?"

She lifted a shoulder. "She was a puppy when I took her. Jerk was abusing her." And she felt no guilt over what she'd done. Kali was hers now. "The last time Enzo dragged me into his office I knew—or thought—he was going to kill me because I didn't have what he wanted. After he gave me an ultimatum he stormed out, his thugs trailing behind him. I scooped up the puppy and shoved her into my bag." She'd been so tiny back then, about six pounds soaking wet. "Kali was so scared, probably because the only thing I'd ever seen him do was kick her or yell at her, so..." She shrugged again, feeling defensive at the way they just stared at her. Tegan might have saved Kali's life, but it went both ways. Her sweet dog had saved Tegan right back. Kali had been her only true friend and companion the last two years. The only constant in her life.

"He could have killed you!" Aaron shouted, a red flush creeping up his neck.

She didn't appreciate the anger. "I wasn't just going to leave her to be abused. And that's not the point." She turned back to the detective.

The other man cleared his throat. "Let's start at the beginning. Like what kind of ultimatum De Fiore gave you, and why he dragged you into his office in the first place. And why you were on the run from him for two years."

Taking a deep breath, she kept her focus on the detective, trying to ignore Aaron's intense stare. "My brother was in the Army, but when he got out he was different. Angry, disillusioned...which isn't really the point, I guess."

She rubbed a hand over her face, pushing down all the painful memories of how distant he'd been when he'd come home. The detective didn't need to know all that. "Anyway, he started drinking and gambling. He got in really deep with the wrong people, had some debts he'd never be able to pay off. So he agreed to do some jobs for De Fiore, transporting stuff. One of those transports was a bunch of stolen diamonds. For all his faults, my brother was well trained and, when he wasn't drinking, highly capable. During the transport, my brother and the diamonds went missing. De Fiore thought I knew where my brother was."

"Do you know?" Detective Duarte asked, his expression neutral.

"No, but I imagine he's dead. He wouldn't have run off with a bunch of diamonds when he would know De Fiore would come after me first. He simply wouldn't have done that." She'd bottled up her pain for a long time, knowing her brother was gone for good.

The detective's mouth pulled into a thin line. "People do crazy stuff for money."

That was true enough, but she knew her older brother wouldn't have left her to fend for herself. Colm had certainly had his faults, just like any other freaking person, but he'd been more into self-destruction than anything else. He wouldn't have let her hang for a crime he committed. "Not him."

Even though she saw a flash of doubt in the detective's eyes, he simply nodded. "So your brother went missing and so did the diamonds."

"Yeah. De Fiore had some of his thugs come and get me as soon as my brother went missing. It's actually the only reason I knew Colm was gone at all. De Fiore told me that if I didn't find my brother or get him to come in with all the stolen diamonds, I'd be dead. I looked for my brother, went to all his haunts—even though I didn't think he would be at any of them." Someone had to have stolen them because Colm simply wouldn't have left her to fend for herself. No way. "The next day someone torched my car with a mannequin inside it. The mannequin had a red wig. The message was pretty damn clear. So I ran."

"Did you go to the cops?" Aaron asked, his voice filled with concern.

She glanced at him and found strength in just looking at him. He might be surly sometimes but he was a solid presence right now. Even if he had just shouted at her, the man made her feel safe. Like nothing could get through him. "There was nothing they could have done to help me. I never saw De Fiore torch my car—or more likely one of his thugs did anyway. I didn't have anything against the man. Not actual *evidence* anyway. I had my word against his, but that's nothing in the legal system. I watch the news, I know how the system works. And everyone in the neighborhood knew the Feds had been after him for years. *Years.* If they didn't have enough evidence to convict him, what would the cops be able to do to protect me when I came to them with nothing but a story that he threatened me? Nothing, that's what."

The detective made a sort of grunting sound that almost sounded like he agreed with her. He would know how the justice system worked. It was like restraining orders. For the most part they were absolutely useless. "How'd you avoid him for two years?"

"After college—before coming back to Chicago—I backpacked for a couple years because I wanted to travel. So basically I just used the same principles from my traveling days and stayed off the grid the best I could. I deleted all my social media accounts, lost contact with everyone I knew, and I used cash everywhere. I got jobs that paid under the table and I didn't stay in one place long."

Constantly moving had worn her down emotionally, though. She'd been tired of looking over her shoulder all the time and having no real connections to people. "When I saw on the news that he'd been murdered, I settled in Miami." For the first couple of months she'd still been off the grid for the most part. Kimmy had paid her under the table until a few months ago when Tegan had finally started to feel safe enough to truly put down roots. But she didn't think the detective needed to know that Kimmy had been paying her in cash in the beginning of her employment.

She cleared her throat. "It's sunny here all the time and the people I've met in Florida up to this point have been so nice. For the first time since I was a kid I feel like I belong somewhere..." Her voice broke and, to her horror, the tears she'd been keeping at bay started pouring out in an unexpected wave. Her throat tightened, making it impossible to talk as emotions strangled her.

She didn't want to go on the run again, didn't want to leave the friends and home she'd made. Before she could swipe the tears away, Aaron had pulled her into his arms. She didn't bother pushing back, but buried her face against his chest and blocked out everything else as sobs racked her body.

She'd been strong for a long time, always trying to keep positive even when she'd been on the run and her only friend had been Kali. Now someone had tried to kill her today. She'd almost died. By all accounts she would have if not for dumb luck. Which meant someone was out there who wanted her dead. Someone who wouldn't simply stop because they'd failed.

At that thought, another sob tore through her and she clutched Aaron's shirt. She was sure she'd be embarrassed later for blubbering all over him but right now she didn't care.

She wasn't sure how long they stayed like that, with him rubbing his big, callused hand down her back and murmuring soothing words she couldn't really make out. She didn't care what the words were anyway. They made her feel better, whatever they were.

Eventually she pulled back, sniffling and, yeah, embarrassed when she saw the tear and mascara stains on his white button-down shirt. "I'm sorry," she muttered.

"Don't be sorry," he murmured as he handed her a box of tissues from the built-in nightstand next to the hospital bed. As she took them she realized the detective was gone.

"Where'd he go?" she asked, swiping at her cheeks and under her eyes, hoping she got the smudges she knew were there.

"He got a call." Aaron was watching her carefully, his expression concerned.

Before she could respond, the detective walked back into the room, his expression even grimmer than it had been before. "Your security company called the department about a breach at your home. Someone broke into your place."

Aaron watched as Tegan's face paled.

"Is someone in my house?" The words came out raspy and trembling.

"Not now. Two officers did a sweep of your place. A picture frame is broken and it's clear someone broke in through the sliding glass door, but they can't tell if anything was taken. No visible electronics are missing so you'll have to do an inspection yourself."

Aaron wanted to pull her into his arms again, to comfort her, but held off for now. "What are you guys going to do about this situation?" he demanded. Because someone tried to kill her today and now her place had been broken into. Not a coincidence.

He planned to call his boss as soon as he could and see if Porter Caldwell could look more into Enzo De Fiore. Or more specifically, if Lizzy Caldwell, Porter's wife, could. The woman was a genius when it came to hacking. She was the best security analyst—aka hacker—they had at Red Stone.

"We're going to keep a detail on her house for now. And I'm going to call the Feds about De Fiore, see if they suspect he might not be dead." Carlito shook his head, clearly frustrated.

That wasn't remotely good enough. "She'll be staying with me until this shit is figured out." Because despite what Tegan seemed to think about him not liking her, she couldn't be further from the truth. She was the first woman he'd been interested in since his wife had left him and their young son almost five years ago. And she terrified the hell out of him. Tegan was a sweet, sexy, smartass woman and she brought out all his protective, possessive instincts. Even if he wasn't insanely attracted to her he'd still have to help. He was involved now and it was clear she didn't have anyone else to help her. He couldn't turn his back on her.

"Um, *she* is right here." Tegan shifted against the crinkly sheets, a frown tugging at her pretty mouth. "That's really nice, Aaron, but I can't stay with you. Someone wants me dead and now someone broke into my place? I'm not bringing that kind of danger to your doorstep—especially because of Dillon."

His chest squeezed that she automatically thought of Dillon. "He'll be staying with my parents and you can stay in my guesthouse. I have a little mother-in-law type suite behind my place. It's a one bedroom, one bath apartment, basically. It's small but no one knows there's a connection between us, because we don't have one.

There are no phone records between us, nothing. You'll be safe."

Her jaw tightened and it was clear she planned to argue more. Well, this was an argument she'd be losing. "It's not happening."

"Fine. Then I'll just stay with you."

She blinked, her mouth opening a fraction. "You can't do that. I won't let you."

"I'll just stay outside your house along with the police detail. Which will make me a target if someone is watching your place."

She stared at him as if he'd lost his mind, so he continued. "Look, I work for one of the best security companies in the country. Maybe the best. I've got eight years' worth of the best training in the world thanks to the Marine Corps, as well as experience in combat zones. I'm fucking trained. You'll be safer with me than anyone else." He knew he was being pushy—he just didn't care. After seeing that explosion with her so close, knowing what could have happened to her, he realized he was a moron for ignoring the spark between them. He wasn't going to let anything happen to her.

"He's right," Duarte said, his voice way calmer than Aaron's. "My former partner is one of the owners at Red Stone. The company does exemplary work. I'm still going to put a detail on your house because I want it under surveillance, but they won't be with you twenty-four-seven. And if there's an emergency in your area and they get a call, they'll have to go. If I were in your shoes, Miss O'Kelly, I'd take Aaron's offer. You can lie low at least for a few days while we investigate this. I'm bringing the

Feds in and we're going to try our hardest to find out who wants you dead. Until we do, the best thing you can do for yourself, for everyone around you, is to hide out where whoever is after you will have no idea to look."

Aaron could freaking kiss the guy right now. Because he could see that the detective's words had an effect on Tegan. Big time.

She bit her bottom lip in the most adorable way. He'd fantasized more than once about nibbling that very lip. He jolted when she looked at him with wide eyes. "Are you really sure?"

He nodded. "Christmas break is just starting for Dillon. He's already asked to stay with my parents for a few days, so this isn't disrupting anyone's schedule." His parents would be thrilled to keep Dillon longer than a couple of days.

"Can I bring my dog?" Her chin jutted out just a little, as if she expected him to say no.

"Yes, of course."

Sighing, she looked back at Duarte. "Can I get my clothes and other stuff from my house?"

He nodded. "We're going to need you to do an inventory of your place anyway to see what, if anything, was taken."

"Okay." Her expression was unreadable as she looked back at Aaron. "I'll stay with you. And thank you, truly. I...I really appreciate it." She swiped at fresh tears and he resisted the urge to do it for her.

No one was going to hurt her again, not if he had anything to do about it. And he was going to make damn sure no one followed them back to his place. They'd have to take precautions leaving the hospital so that they weren't seen together if anyone was watching. He mentally started making plans for how to do just that.

CHAPTER FOUR

"If you keep giving her treats she'll never leave you alone," Tegan said to Dillon. Callan had just dropped Dillon off and Aaron was somewhere talking to his brother while Tegan and Dillon hung out in the kitchen with Kali.

The adorable five-year-old wasn't doing a very good job of hiding how many treats he was giving to Kali under the kitchen table.

He turned to look at her with dark, amber-flecked eyes so similar to his father's, his expression intent. "I don't want her to leave me alone."

The kid was always so dang serious. "Well, I think she'll play with you whether you give her treats or not. She's always so excited to see you at the shop. And she's not like that with everyone."

Kali thumped her tail against the kitchen floor and actually *nodded*, as if to reiterate Tegan's point. She swore that dog was half human some days. *Most* days.

Dillon grinned widely. "Really?"

"Really."

Kali jumped up onto Dillon's seat, placing one paw on his leg and one on the chair. She kissed Dillon's face, making the boy giggle and wrap his arms around her neck. "Do you think I could have ice cream?" he asked, his voice muffled against Kali's neck.

The sweet husky was soaking up the attention as usual.

Tegan pushed her chair back and was glad she didn't feel nauseous. The doctor had said it might be a possibility but other than a low-grade headache she actually felt okay. "Sure. What kind do you guys have?"

"Vanilla and chocolate swirl is my favorite."

"No ice cream until after dinner." Aaron's deep, sexy voice was only mildly exasperated as he stepped into the kitchen. He'd long since ditched his jacket and was wearing dark slacks and a white button-down shirt with the sleeves rolled up to his elbows—showing off all sorts of sinewy, hard muscles. The man was way too sexy.

"Come on, Dad! Tegan said it was okay."

His eyebrows arched. "Only because she doesn't know the rules."

Tegan inwardly winced, realizing she'd made a mistake. Of course a kid couldn't just have ice cream in the middle of the afternoon. Or she guessed they couldn't. He'd need vegetables and stuff like that. Yeah, she wasn't ready to be a mom anytime soon. Another reminder that Aaron wasn't the guy for her, because he and Dillon were a package deal, no doubt about it. And she didn't know the first thing about kids. Other than they were a little terrifying.

"Sorry," she murmured.

Aaron shrugged, clearly not annoyed if the sexy half smile on his face was any indication. "He still tries it with his uncle Callan and anyone he thinks will give him what he wants."

"Nana always gives me..." Dillon's dark eyes widened. "Hey, can we get a dog, Dad?"

Smooth topic change, Tegan thought, fighting a smile.

"We'll talk about it," Aaron said to him before looking back at Tegan. "Callan's going to hang out at Kimmy's shop the next couple days and keep an eye on the place."

"Thank God." Tegan had been worried about that. Just because she wouldn't be at the shop didn't mean that someone looking for her wouldn't come by ready to finish what they'd started. "Maybe Callan will finally work up the courage to ask her out."

Aaron's mouth lifted into another one of those devastating half smiles. It was like he'd been holding onto all this sexiness for eight months and was now letting her see a softer side to him. It was irresistible. Almost. Because she had to resist the man. "God, I hope so. Put us all out of our misery."

She laughed. Callan and Kimmy pretty much danced around their attraction to each other to the point of being ridiculous. Kimmy was a widow and a single mom, so Tegan could understand her hesitance in being in a relationship, but it was pretty clear Callan would do anything for her. She couldn't understand why he was so gun shy.

"Look, my mom will be here soon. We'll talk when we're alone." Talking about any of this in front of Dillon wasn't a good idea. She wondered if Aaron knew more from the detective.

After leaving the hospital she'd had a police escort to her place where she'd packed up a bag of clothes, her laptop, and then Kali from her neighbor's house. From there she'd thought she'd have another police escort but instead someone from the company Aaron worked for— Red Stone Security—had picked her up with Aaron already inside. They'd driven to Red Stone, changed vehicles, then their driver had driven them around for over an hour before stopping at Aaron's place even though he didn't live very far from her. Their driver had assured her that no one had tried to follow them. She felt a lot better being here with all the precautions they'd taken.

At the sound of a doorbell chime Kali let out a short yip and raced out of the room, her nails clicking against the tile. Dillon wasn't far behind her.

"She can get a little excited." She couldn't help the apologetic note in her voice. Tegan knew dogs weren't for everyone and Kali was excited to be in a new place. So far she'd been pretty well behaved but she was still loud and jumpy. At least soon Tegan would be able to get her settled into the guesthouse, which was way smaller. Once it was just Tegan and Kali, she figured her dog would calm down a little.

Aaron frowned slightly, falling in step with her. "I had a couple dogs growing up. She's not a problem at all. Okay?"

Tegan released a sigh she hadn't realized she'd been holding. She felt weird being here, like she had to watch her step. It wasn't Aaron's doing. If anything he seemed to be going out of his way to make sure she was comfortable. It was a huge change from the closed-off man who'd been coming into Kimmy's shop the last eight months. "Okay, thanks. I just feel weird, I guess. I don't want to get in your way or anything."   —

He frowned again, but turned away from her as they reached the foyer. Bree Fitzpatrick, his mother and a friend of Tegan's, was scooping Dillon into a giant hug. Dillon was trying to whisper—and failing—about getting ice cream as soon as they left.

Tegan bit back another smile when Aaron let out an exasperated sigh. Seeing him in full-on dad mode was really, really nice. She'd always thought of him as this intimidating, cranky—and ridiculously sexy—man. Now he just seemed like a sexy, take-charge, do-the-right-thing kind of guy. Seriously, he didn't know her that well but was still offering up his house because she was in danger. In her experience, the world didn't work that way. Which made her want him even more. It was stupid, because she wasn't looking for a relationship and definitely not with a ready-made family.

"Tegan! I heard about what happened." Bree moved at her lightning fast, pulling her into a tight hug. The woman was in her sixties with dark hair, petite, fit, and a force of nature.

She hugged Bree back, glad to see her. Tegan's own mother had been lacking in the maternal department, so whenever she was around Bree, she found herself wishing she'd had a mom like her growing up. "I'm okay," she said, stepping back. It wasn't true. She was a hot mess inside but the answer was instinctive. She didn't want to admit that she was filled with terror that someone wanted her dead bad enough to set a bomb in her car right in the middle of a busy street. "Thanks to your son."

Aaron just grunted and gave his mom a hug. Bree was still shaking her head as she stepped back. "I can't believe what happened. No one can. Neither of you have been named, but it's been all over the news about the bombing."

The neighborhood where Kimmy's shop was located was pretty tight knit. Some of the shops had experienced turnovers in the last few years, according to Kimmy, but it was rare. It wasn't a touristy part of Miami, but a friendly local one, where families had been for generations. Kimmy's was one of the newer places but it was doing well. Part of Tegan was sad that she wouldn't get to go into work but she didn't want to bring any danger to the shop. At least she had her website design projects to work on. It would keep her busy and focused—and hopefully keep her mind off the person who had targeted her to die. Though Tegan knew nothing could do that. Not really. She wouldn't be able to focus until the person was caught.

Bree pointed to a big brown bag by the front door. "The Mederos family sent over a bunch of food for you. I told them I'd be seeing you so they fixed up enough food for three days."

The Mederos family owned Montez's Grill and one of their daughters ran a lingerie boutique on the same street as Kimmy's place. Tegan knew all of them. Everyone had been so welcoming when she started working for Kimmy and she'd redone almost all the websites for everyone on the street at a discount. She knew that people cared, but this act of giving was just too much on her emotional state right now.

Tears pricked Tegan's eyes and she inwardly cursed as she swiped at them. She'd barely cried in the last couple of years. There had been no time in her life for feeling sorry for herself, only survival. Now... "Damn it," she muttered as the floodgates stayed open. "I'm normally not a crier."

Bree pulled her into another hug and patted her back gently. "You're holding up better than I would. I'm glad you decided to show some sense and stay here. If you get tired of my son you can stay at my place."

Laughing, she said, "Thank you." Tears finally dried up, Tegan stepped back. God, Aaron probably thought she was a total basket case by now. Which didn't matter anyway, since she didn't care what he thought. Which was a total lie.

"If you want, I can take Kali off your hands," Dillon piped in.

"What?"

"I can take Kali to Nana's tonight." He gave her the sweetest smile that had just a hint of mischievousness.

"That's a great idea, Dillon. Let's give Tegan a chance to rest. We haven't had a dog in the house in years." Bree gently petted Kali's head and Kali, as always, soaked up the attention.

"Oh no, she'll stay here. She's already in a new place and taking her somewhere else might stress her out." And Tegan wasn't sure she wanted to be away from her sweet dog anyway.

Kali whined. Next to Dillon she was practically vibrating with energy as she tried to sit still. She wasn't doing a very good job, her butt and tail wagging, moving her entire body.

Dillon placed his little hand on Kali's head. "Nana's got a fenced-in yard so she can go out and poop anytime she needs. Then tonight she can sleep with me. In my bed." He looked incredibly excited at the thought.

"I don't know..." She looked at Aaron, hoping he'd say something.

He just lifted his eyebrows and shrugged. "I've learned that when the two of them gang up together, it's a good idea to just say yes."

Tegan looked back at Bree. "Bree, Kali can be a lot to handle—"

"If she's too much we'll just bring her back over here. We only live a couple blocks away. We're in the same neighborhood."

"Oh." Well, that made her feel better. "Are you sure?" Kali was a good dog, but Bree and her husband were older. Tegan was worried she might be too much to handle. And she felt weird being away from her dog. Kali was always a comfort.

"Absolutely. I'll just need her leash and food and we'll be fine. I've still got Bandit's old dog bed and toys, so she'll be fine. And my house is all tile and wood so even if she has an accident it's no big deal. I'll bring her back in the morning on my walk. You need some rest. Take advantage of this."

Tegan looked at Kali, torn. "You want to go with Dillon?"

She barked in answer then licked Dillon's face before trotting over to Tegan and jumping up on her to kiss her as well. Yes, that dog was definitely part human.

Okay then, it was settled. Tegan scratched behind her ear. "Just let me get her stuff." Tegan felt lost letting her dog go but she was too emotional to put up much of an argument and it was clear Dillon really wanted to spend time with her. Considering Aaron was giving her a safe place to sleep, she wasn't going to complain.

She headed for the kitchen to grab Kali's stuff.

"You really don't have to let her go," Aaron said quietly behind her.

She nearly jumped as she picked up Kali's bag of food, toys, and leash from one of the kitchen chairs. She hadn't realized he'd followed her. "I know, but it's hard to say no to either of them. And Dillon looks so excited at the thought of getting to play with her."

Aaron's mouth curved up. "Yeah, he's been begging me for a dog for about six months now."

"I don't know how you ever say no to him."

He snorted. "It'll get easier, trust me."

"If you say so." She lifted the bag but he immediately took it from her.

The gesture warmed her from the inside out even as she reminded herself that Aaron was not for her. He had a kid, and even though she adored kids, they were a huge responsibility. Plus, she knew that Aaron had been hurt in the past. She might not know all the details but she'd heard Kimmy say enough that she'd managed to put some of the pieces together. She knew that things hadn't worked out between him and his ex-wife. She wasn't really sure of the why, though.

Not that any of that mattered. Even if Tegan had been looking for a relationship, he wasn't the type of man she wanted. Except maybe in the sexiness department, because in that one he was off the charts.

* * *

"I think they made more than three days' worth of food," Aaron said, hefting the takeout bags the Mederos family had sent over. Relief slid through him that Dillon was at his parents' and completely safe. He was also very aware that he was now alone with Tegan. Months ago he would have hated that. Now he could finally admit to himself how much he wanted her.

"Whatever's in there, I could probably eat all of it right now. I didn't even think I was hungry," Tegan murmured, heading into the kitchen with him.

"You've had a lot happen today. Eating and sleeping are the best things you can do." He knew from experience that sometimes sleep was the only damn thing that could help.

"I'll be okay to sleep with the mild concussion, right?"

"Yeah. Enough time's passed and you're not exhibiting any signs of being concussed but...I think you should sleep in my guest room instead of the guesthouse." He didn't look at her as he spoke, just set the food on the counter and pulled out the top two boxes. He was prepared for her to argue so he continued. "It'll be easier for me to keep one house locked down from any potential threat and I'll be able to wake you up easier as well. I don't know that I even need to but I'll feel better waking you up a couple times tonight, just in case."

He looked up as she pulled out one of the chairs at the island. She raised an eyebrow. "Was that your plan all along, to have me stay at the house?"

"Yeah." Why bother to deny it?

She snorted. "You really are like Bree."

His mouth curved up at that. "Why do you say that?" He grabbed a water bottle from the fridge and slid it across to her.

"She plans on things and just expects everyone to go along with her. She's a bulldozer when she wants to be."

"I didn't realize you two had spent much time together." More than anything he was surprised his mother hadn't said anything about spending time with Tegan. He knew her from Kimmy's shop but his mom hadn't mentioned Tegan other than in passing.

"I redesigned a few websites for some of the charities she volunteers at and I've seen her in action. She gets people to agree to stuff and makes them think it was their idea to start with. And she comes into the shop a lot. I think she's just as frustrated with Callan as everyone else. I once heard her on the phone telling someone that Kimmy would be her daughter-in-law if her son could just pull his head out of his butt."

"I have a feeling you're using nicer language than she did," he said dryly.

She let out a short laugh. "I am. Your mom's feisty." She paused. "Can I ask you something personal?"

With his back to her, he pulled out a couple of plates for dinner. Inwardly he braced for the inevitable questions about his ex. "Sure."

"You said you were in the Marines. Did you ever— and if this is too personal, feel free to ignore me—but you must have seen gunfire and explosions and..."

Surprised, he turned to find her staring at him, looking miserable. He wasn't sure where she was going with the conversation but it wasn't what he'd expected. Normally he didn't talk about his time overseas. Not to civilians anyway. They always wanted to ask jackass questions, like had he killed anyone or how many people he had killed. Like it was any of their fucking business. It was clear she wasn't asking him questions out of a morbid sense of curiosity, though.

He set the plates down and went to sit next to her. "What are you trying to ask?" he said, taking one of her hands in his. Her skin was soft. She let out a little shiver and he didn't think it was because she was cold.

"I honestly don't know. I feel like a mess right now. I know you must have seen way worse stuff than a car bomb so I feel stupid even talking about it. I'm just feeling off kilter, I guess. Really off balance. Whenever I close my eyes, all I can see, feel, and hear is the explosion. And if I let myself really think about what could have happened, I break out into a sweat." She pulled her hand free, wrapped her arms around herself, and started to shiver.

Fuck it. He pulled her into his arms, not stopping at a simple hug. Some intrinsic part of him needed to make this better for her, needed to take away all the bullshit.

He tugged her right into his lap, much to her surprise if the little yelp she let out was any indication.

Her petite frame fit perfectly against him. She curled up to him, still shaking a little, but not too badly as he tightened his grip. She laid her head on his chest, letting him hold her. "It's scary to think that I could have been in the car or right next to it when it blew."

"It's going to be scary for a while. You might have nightmares about it." He certainly had. Occasionally he still did. That shit never went away. Not truly.

Sighing, she didn't respond.

"I think you'll be okay, though." After everything she'd told Duarte and him about being on the run from a gangster for two years, he had a lot of respect for her. That kind of life was hard, and she'd handled herself well because she was still here. She was a survivor and she hadn't let her life get her down.

The Marines had been tough and he'd spent a lot of years in the worst shitholes, but he'd always had his men, people watching out for him. She'd had no one and he hated that. Even if it was stupid, he was determined to be the one who had her back now. Even though he didn't want to analyze exactly why he was so determined to keep her safe and close to him. Because she was the kind of woman who could destroy him if he let her in.

She sighed again. "I will. I'm just feeling a little sorry for myself right now."

"You're allowed to." Her sweet scent teased him. Whatever shampoo she used was subtle, some sort of vanilla and lavender combination. Holding her close like this was something he'd imagined countless times, though under very different circumstances—naked ones.

Ever since he'd met her all those months ago he'd been drawn to her. She had such a sunny disposition and a lot of sass. She was the opposite of his ex in every way. He hadn't wanted to be attracted to Tegan, hadn't wanted to be attracted to anyone after what he'd gone through. Now he was losing the fight to keep his distance from her.

He cleared his throat. "Listen, the past few months I might have been kinda...grumpy."

She laughed and pulled back to look at him. Only inches separated them and it took all his willpower not to drop his gaze to her mouth and the very kissable, full lips he'd fantasized about far too often. "That's a bit of an understatement. Why are you like that with me? And don't say it's with everyone because you're nice to Kimmy. But you always seemed annoyed with me—until today."

"I'm nice to Kimmy because Callan would kill me if I looked at her the wrong way."

Her lips curved up. "True enough. So what's the deal?"

He wanted to slide her back to her seat because having this conversation with her on his lap was making it hard to think, knowing exactly how close she was to his cock, how easy it would be to shift positions and...nope. He shut that thought right down. Not that it did much since he was still getting hard. How could he not be with her sitting on his lap like this? "You might know that I was married before?"

Tegan nodded, her blue eyes unreadable.

"After Dillon was born, she split. Signed over all parental rights to me and left town. Said she wanted nothing to do with either of us, that she hated my family and hated Miami." He'd had a lot of bitterness about it for a long time. But he'd let it go because he couldn't be a good parent and be angry all the time. Dillon deserved better than that. His son was going to get the best of everything he had to offer, nothing less.

Tegan's eyes widened. "Seriously?"

He nodded.

She blinked once. "I can understand divorce, but leaving your kid like that?"

His jaw tightened. "She was...she had issues." He'd been young and in lust with her when they'd met. He'd been in the Corps and she'd been sexy and all about him. Or so he'd thought. He'd just been young and stupid, seeing what he wanted to see instead of what was really there: a selfish woman who'd only cared about herself. And Dillon had paid the price for it. "She died of a drug overdose about a year after she left. Somewhere out west."

"Wow. I'm sorry."

He was just sorry that he'd one day have to explain to his son what had happened to his mother. He cleared his throat, finally getting to his point. "You're her opposite and...the first woman I've been interested in in about five years." He couldn't believe he was even admitting this to her, but he felt compelled to. Felt as if he needed to explain to her why he'd been so distant because he wanted to start fresh, maybe start something with her.

"I didn't handle being around you well." Mainly because he hadn't trusted his instincts around women. But after seeing Tegan in action with customers, seeing the way she was with his son, and now after hearing all that she'd been through, he knew she was nothing like his ex. And he wasn't the same boy who'd fallen for the wrong kind of woman.

Tegan's eyes widened and her lips parted ever so slightly.

Against his will, his gaze dipped to those lips and all he wanted to do was kiss her, taste what he'd been fantasizing about for so damn long.

She hadn't responded to his admission but when her tongue flicked out against her bottom lip, he groaned, unable to stop the reaction.

The air was suddenly too heavy and she felt way too good in his arms. He started to lean closer when the buzz of his cell phone in his pocket made them both jump.

She blinked as if coming out of a daze then slid off his lap as though she couldn't move fast enough. He wanted to ignore the call, but it could be Duarte or an emergency with Dillon. As a father, he never ignored his phone.

When he saw it was just one of his friends from work, he ignored it. Not that it mattered. Whatever might have happened between him and Tegan clearly wasn't going to now. She'd moved around the island and was looking at the food he'd laid out, clearly avoiding his gaze and putting solid distance between them.

Part of him was relieved nothing had happened. Getting involved with her was a risk he wasn't sure he was willing to take.

CHAPTER FIVE

Tegan stared at the ceiling of the guest room, replaying Aaron's words over in her head. She couldn't believe he was interested in her. Considering his behavior today she actually *could*, but it was hard to reconcile this change with the man who'd seemed perpetually annoyed with her over the last eight months.

After everything he'd admitted about his ex, she hadn't been sure how to respond. Heck, she still wasn't sure. She wanted Aaron, no doubt about that, but talk about some serious baggage. And she had her own issues as well. She'd been a military brat, and then after her dad died, her mom had dragged her and her brother to a place they hated and had barely been present in their lives. Tegan knew absolutely nothing about kids. She wasn't the right type of woman for Aaron. He should want someone sweeter, more nurturing. Someone...not her.

Getting involved would be stupid—

She sat up at the sound of a doorbell downstairs. The two-story house had a simple layout: kitchen, living room, dining room, and family room downstairs, and four bedrooms upstairs. The place was huge, not to mention the guesthouse apartment out back.

Even though she doubted a would-be assassin would take the time to ring the doorbell, a jolt of panic punched through her all the same.

When she peeked out into the hallway she could hear Aaron disarming the alarm system downstairs. That meant he recognized whoever was on the other side of the door. Still, a low-grade panic hummed through her, refusing to settle until she knew who was there.

A moment later she heard the sound of the front door opening and then came Detective Duarte's voice. She was wearing yoga pants and a T-shirt, so she grabbed a sweater and pulled it over her head since she didn't have a bra on, and hurried downstairs. The fact that the detective was here in the middle of the night was *not* good news. She held back the fear and worry because freaking out before knowing exactly why he'd shown up instead of calling wouldn't do anyone any good.

Aaron was talking quietly to the detective in the foyer when she joined them. Duarte was still wearing a suit, though no tie. Even close to midnight the man looked polished and put together. His gray eyes were startling against his bronze skin and she had a feeling he never wanted for female company.

Still, compared to Aaron, the man did nothing for her. Aaron had more of an edge to him. His dark military-style short hair only highlighted all the hard planes of his face, making him all the more interesting to look at. When he'd told her she was the first woman he'd been interested in over the last five years, she wondered if he'd slept with anyone since his ex. It seemed crazy to think he'd been celibate because, come on, look at the man. But she didn't want to think about him getting physical with someone else anyway. It made something annoyingly possessive flare to life. She wasn't used to it and wasn't sure she liked it.

She cleared her throat. "What's wrong?" Because a detective wasn't stopping by at midnight to chat about the weather and she couldn't do any stupid small talk. She simply didn't have it in her.

"I just had a conversation with the FBI agent who was head of the team to bring down De Fiore right before he allegedly died."

Allegedly? Oh, that was *not* good. The word slammed through her, making it hard to breathe for a moment. She looked at Aaron, needing someone to ground her right now. Because all she wanted to do was grab her stuff, her dog, and run.

His expression was hard, but she knew it wasn't directed at her. "Let's take this into the kitchen."

"Do you have decaf coffee?" she asked Aaron as they entered the kitchen.

He looked at her as if she'd lost her mind. "No point in drinking coffee if it doesn't have caffeine."

A slight smile curved her lips. "What about caffeine-free tea?" Because she needed something warm and soothing that wouldn't keep her up all night.

He shook his head. "How about hot chocolate?"

It was hard to imagine a man like Aaron drinking hot chocolate because it seemed so impractical but he did have a five-year-old. There would be a little caffeine in it, but she didn't care. "Sounds perfect, thanks." Feeling shaky as he started moving around the kitchen, she turned to the detective, a heavy ball of stress tangled in her stomach. "So, allegedly dead?" The question left a sour taste in her mouth.

Duarte pulled out a chair at the island so she did the same and sat next to him. "I'll keep this short, but yes, *allegedly* dead. The FBI was looking into him before he 'died.' They have an airtight case against him. Tax fraud and evasion."

She snorted. "Just like Capone?"

"Exactly. They were about to move on him when he suddenly got murdered."

That seemed convenient. "What about the body, though? Wouldn't they have to confirm that it was him?"

"Yes, and that's where it gets a little tricky. The body was burned beyond recognition. The dental records match but that just means the records match whoever's are on file. He could have paid off someone for that. And..." Duarte sighed, his grayish eyes grim. "There was an issue with the DNA sample taken. It got corrupted during testing—which they believe was intentional. Right around the same time there was a snafu that released the body, which was cremated immediately. So they didn't have anything left to test."

Ice slid through her veins, striking at all her nerve endings with sharp pricks. None of this had been public information or she'd have never settled down in Miami. Even then she'd waited to put down roots because she'd been afraid De Fiore had been somehow waiting to trap her. This sounded way too sketchy. "That feels like a bit of a coincidence."

"Exactly. But without more proof, they can't make a case that he's not dead. He hasn't resurfaced anywhere so if he really is alive, he's basically living off the grid. They want him bad, but can't expend a bunch of resources hunting a ghost who may or may not be dead."

She rubbed a hand over her face, feeling about a thousand years old. "So he's back for those stupid diamonds. Well, he's in for a big disappointment."

Duarte nodded as Aaron slid a steaming mug in front of her. He'd even put whipped cream on top. The sight warmed her heart.

"Thank you," she murmured, glad he was here with her. She might not know him very well, but the man was solid. After what she'd recently learned about his military experience, it was clear he was the kind of man you wanted on your side. Not only that, but he'd stepped up and taken over as a single father, and it was clear that he thought his kid hung the moon. He was a good man. She couldn't fight the guilt weighing on her that she'd brought her troubles to his doorstep. It made her wonder if she should cut and run. For the first time in years she wanted to stay in one place. Wanted it so desperately it was a live thing inside her.

"The diamonds..." Duarte said, drawing her attention back to him. "I don't know if this is about them."

"What else could it be about?" She didn't have any other enemies. None that she knew about anyway. And nothing that warranted the kind of violence from yesterday.

"Honestly, I don't know. I just think it would be pretty stupid of him to try to kill you *before* he got what he wanted. And according to my FBI contact, bombs aren't really his style. He likes to get up close and personal."

The iciness spread, wrapping around her insides and chilling her straight to the bone. Why hadn't she thought of that? It didn't actually make sense for De Fiore to want to kill her. Not yet anyway. Not until he got what he wanted—except she didn't have anything to give him.

"The Feds want to talk to you. They know who your brother is but they didn't realize there was a tie to you and De Fiore or they'd have come to you sooner. They wanted to talk to you tonight but I wouldn't tell them where you're staying. Said I'd bring you in tomorrow morning for a sit down with them. If you want."

She didn't particularly want to talk to more law enforcement and she had a feeling Duarte was just being polite and giving her the illusion of a choice. She'd have to talk to the Feds one way or another. "I'll do it. Thanks for not dragging me down to see them tonight." Under other circumstances she figured they would have tracked her down, but she'd turned off her cell phone and taken out the battery at Aaron's insistence. He said no one should be able to track her without access to her phone.

Duarte's mouth curved up slightly and he shrugged. "You should be rested when you talk to them. It'll be in my office, not in an interrogation room. And if they start pushing you, tell them you want to talk to me or a lawyer. Don't let them railroad you into anything. They can't keep you against your will."

She blinked, surprised by his heated tone. "What could they possibly railroad me into?"

"Don't know that they will. But I know how they operate. They're pushy when they want to be, even to victims. If you start to feel uncomfortable about any line of questioning, end the conversation. You're a victim, not a suspect. Sometimes the Feds need a reminder of stuff like that." There was a hint of derision in his voice.

Grateful for the warning, she nodded. "I'll keep that in mind."

He pushed up and nodded at Aaron, who'd been quiet. "Eight o'clock tomorrow work for you?"

"We'll be there." Aaron's expression was unreadable as he tilted his chin toward the front of the house.

She quickly realized he meant for Duarte to follow him to the door. Tegan didn't bother going with them. If Aaron wanted privacy with Duarte, she wouldn't intrude.

She wrapped her hands around the mug but it didn't do much to warm her. Not when chills snaked through her body.

She hadn't thought De Fiore would fake his own death. Sure, the thought had entered her mind that his death wasn't real, but it had been eight months. And she'd come back onto the grid, so to speak, about three months ago—even if she had settled in Miami eight months ago.

De Fiore had been head of his own little criminal empire but seemingly untouchable. Now to learn he was quite possibly alive? She slid off her chair, that familiar fear grasping her in its sharp talons.

She should run. Far, far away. She'd done it before, and she could go off the grid again. Except now it would hurt worse than before. Chicago had never felt like home. Nowhere their mother had dragged them after her dad's death had really felt like home. After college, and then her years of traveling, Tegan had just gone back to Chicago because it had been familiar and her brother had been living there. She'd never planned to settle down there permanently. When she'd gone on the run she hadn't cared about leaving the city. If anything, leaving behind all those painful memories had been easy. Like cutting away a gangrenous part of her life.

Now would be different. She loved Miami and more than that, she loved the people she'd gotten to know. She'd allowed herself to start putting down roots, to make friends.

"You're not going anywhere." Aaron's deep voice pulled her out of her thoughts.

Blinking, she realized he was standing on the other side of the island, watching her. She hadn't even heard him return to the kitchen. "What?"

"I see the look on your face. Your instinct is telling you to run. Well, you're not going to." There was no room for argument in his voice, in those commanding words.

She wanted to deny what she'd been thinking, but lifted a shoulder. "Maybe it would be better if I did run." Even if it was the last thing she truly wanted to do. Going on the run drained her in ways she hated thinking about. The last couple of years before settling in Miami she'd been a muted version of herself, always worried, always looking over her shoulder. "Because if it's not De Fiore who wants to kill me, then I'm screwed. I mean, I'm screwed either way but at least if he's the one after me I know what he looks like. Now I'm fighting a ghost, because I have no idea who else could want me dead."

And she was making anyone associated with her a target. Sure, she was relatively safe. For the moment. But it wouldn't last. She couldn't hide at Aaron's forever. Even if they'd taken a ridiculous amount of precautions, maybe there was something they hadn't seen, an angle they hadn't thought of. She shut that thought down before she started hyperventilating. Giving in to fear was weak. She had to keep a steady head.

"Let the FBI and the Miami PD do their job. At least let them investigate this before doing something stupid. The bombing just happened. They're putting all their resources into this."

His tone and the word *stupid* rankled her. "I can take care of myself." She'd been doing it for a long time.

"I know. Doesn't mean you should run. Stay here where you're safe. No one could possibly know where you are right now. There's been no leak to the news of the names of the witnesses, no leak that I was there. There's no fucking link between us." His voice was heated, his expression determined. "And if here stops being safe, we'll figure something else out. I work for a powerful company. They'll help you if the cops can't."

"I...don't think I can afford their help." She didn't know much about the company he worked for but he wore expensive suits, drove a nice truck, and lived in a very nice area. Not to mention she'd seen the Red Stone

Security building downtown. That place had been intimidating and seriously prime real estate.

He frowned. "They'll likely do it for free. If they don't, I'll pay."

She shook her head. "Why would they do that?" She wasn't going to ask why he'd offered to pay, only because she didn't want to insult him. And she didn't want the answer. She wasn't letting him pay to help her, period. He'd already done too much.

"Because you need help."

She wanted to tell him that the world didn't work that way but his very determined expression said that he meant every word. Something about the look in his eyes was too intense, too...something. She didn't want to analyze it or what it made her feel. Aaron was not the man for her. She had to keep reminding herself of that. "So eight o'clock tomorrow?" Or today, really. It was after midnight after all.

He nodded. "I'll drive you."

"Are you sure you can take off work like this?" They hadn't actually talked about that. He'd pretty much told her that he was helping her and just taken over. She was grateful for that but didn't want to interfere with his life—or put him or anyone else in danger.

"Yep." He was watching her with that unnerving intensity.

"Are you going to expand on that?"

"What's to expand? I've got time and I'm taking it. We're going to get this mess figured out one way or another." As he spoke he rounded the island so that he was a couple of feet from her.

His proximity and the way he said *we* did something strange to her insides. It was like now that he'd decided to admit his attraction and go all protective he'd let down some sort of wall between them. She wasn't sure how she felt about it. "Okay. Well, thank you." She slid off the chair, her hot chocolate mostly untouched. She'd needed the warmth but her stomach was too tied up to handle much—and she needed space from him. Right now she was feeling weak where he was concerned. Getting involved with Aaron would be monumentally stupid for her heart.

His spicy scent teased her as he looked down at her, and she fought the instinct to lean in to him, to touch him. Her nipples pebbled under that intense stare, making her glad she'd put on a sweater.

His closeness wasn't helping her reaction to him either.

"What?" she asked when he just watched her.

"Just wondering if you're ever going to respond to what I told you earlier." His voice was deep, curling around her, pulling her in and making her feel stupidly secure.

Something she couldn't afford to feel. Not now.

She didn't need for him to specify what he meant. In fact, if he said the actual words again, told her that he was attracted to her, she wasn't sure she could handle it. She cleared her throat. "I don't know what to say. Right now isn't really a good time for me to think of...anything related to...stuff."

A hint of amusement danced in his dark eyes. "Stuff?" He took a step closer, minimizing the distance between them. It was subtle but he was crowding her personal space.

Forget being chilled. Heat spilled through her and she felt her cheeks start to warm as she looked up at him. Had he always been so broad, so tall? "Yes. Stuff. Between you and me." Gah, why did her voice have to tremble?

Before she realized what he intended, he was cupping her cheek, his hold so gentle and sweet she had to resist leaning into it. Oh so softly, he rubbed his thumb against her cheek. A shiver rolled through her. "Now's not a good time. I get it, but...I'm interested. And I'm not going anywhere."

His deeply spoken words rolled over her, enveloping her. Since she couldn't find her voice she just nodded. He was simply putting it all out there, telling her he was interested. But that could mean any number of things. He was probably just interested in sex.

The truth was she was, too. More than sex, though. She didn't want something casual, not with a man like Aaron. But...no. She simply didn't have time to think about sex or relationships or anything else. Not tonight. Not when she had a meeting with a federal agent in the morning to talk about the probably not-so-dead gangster or someone else who might be trying to kill her. That thought was enough to douse her with metaphorical cold water.

"I'm going to reset the alarm." Aaron dropped his hand, his gaze still all-consuming as he took a step back from her, giving her the space she desperately needed.

The second he did it was like she could breathe again. She sucked air into her lungs as he strode from the kitchen. Even the way he walked was sexy.

Sighing, she rubbed a hand over her face. She needed sleep. Unfortunately, she had a feeling it wasn't going to come easy. Not tonight.

* * *

Sticking to the low speed limit, Alec Rossi drove down Tegan O'Kelly's quiet residential street. Cute little townhomes and bungalows lined the curving road, and most vehicles were in the driveways and out of sight. Some kids' toys had been left in front yards, but for the most part all the yards were neat and tidy. The majority of homes had Christmas lights adorning them or at least a wreath on the front door and festive ribbons on the mailbox. It was late, after midnight, but the neighborhood was big enough that it wasn't strange to see someone driving home.

Of course he wasn't going home. He didn't live here.

When Alec saw an unmarked cop car in Tegan's driveway he kept driving. Hers was one of the few homes without decorations or lights. He cracked his knuckles, frustrated by the extra security. But it was to be expected after the bombing. If there hadn't been anyone outside her place he would have been even more suspicious.

There were two entrances to the neighborhood so he used the other to leave instead of heading back down the street. If he did the latter, just circling back by the cop car, it would draw attention he didn't need. For all the cop knew, he lived here, and Alec didn't want the guy to see him twice.

Not in this vehicle anyway. He'd have to ditch it now and procure another one.

The O'Kelly woman was making things difficult for him by not doing what she was supposed to: die. It wasn't personal and if she wanted to blame anyone it was that stupid prick Enzo De Fiore.

Enzo should have stayed dead. He had enough money to get out of the country. Or he should have had enough if he was smart. All those years as top dog, the man should have been squirreling away funds. But Enzo thought the woman had a bunch of diamonds and wanted them, had refused to leave the country without them.

Too bad for Enzo she didn't have jack.

Unfortunately for the woman, she needed to die because of Enzo's belief. She was a loose end and her death had to be violent and spectacular. To make it look like her nonexistent partner had killed her.

That way Enzo would just walk away. She'd be dead and, without any leads, the fool wouldn't have anyone to hunt anymore. He would leave the country and be out of their hair. Or he'd just keep hunting her imaginary partner until he got caught by the Feds.

Of course, Alec could just kill Enzo and be done with it, but his boss didn't want him to do that. Not unless he had to.

Stupid code of honor or whatever. Alec didn't agree with it, but that was just the way it was with these old school gangsters sometimes. They had rules they liked to follow. At least when it suited them. Because if Enzo got in the way, Alec knew his boss would order him to kill the guy.

Hell, he might kill Enzo regardless. Just because he could. He could make that one look like an accident. Or just kill him and dispose of the body so that no one would find it.

It was certainly something to think about.

Glancing in the rearview mirror, he saw that he wasn't being tailed so he started heading back to his temporary residence.

The good news was, if the woman had a police detail on her place, she was home. Or it was more likely that she was. Nothing could stop Alec when he was on a job, so a little thing like a bodyguard outside wouldn't save her.

He'd just have to break in and kill her. Then set her house on fire, making sure the entire place was razed to the ground. It was one option.

Tomorrow he'd head to where she worked and see if he could get to her there. Unfortunately, if she had a police detail it would make his life more difficult.

Which was just as well. His jobs had started to get boring anyway. Livening things up a little wasn't such a bad thing.

He just wished he knew for certain if the woman was home. He'd tried tracking her phone but couldn't get a ping on it. She'd probably taken out the battery.

Something he found very interesting. Most people wouldn't have thought to do that.

But she *had* been on the run from Enzo for a couple of years so she was adept at hiding. Clearly. Going off grid the way she had would have been difficult for most people. But humans could do amazing things in an effort to stay alive. The survival instinct in some was a powerful thing. Maybe taking out the battery was a habit she'd picked up. Alec just hoped she didn't go on the run again.

Because if she did, Enzo would try to track her and he'd have to track her, too. All he wanted to do was wrap up this job and head home. Not hunt after some bitch who should already be dead.

CHAPTER SIX

Aaron crossed his arms over his chest as he leaned against the wall outside Carlito's office. He couldn't hear anything going on inside other than the murmur of voices. He didn't like that Tegan was in there without him. At least Carlito had insisted on being in there—and he'd been stubborn about it, too—because the Feds had wanted to speak to her alone.

Aaron understood why he'd told Tegan not to let the FBI bulldoze her, because that was exactly their MO. When he'd been in the Corps he hadn't dealt with them, but since working for Red Stone he'd had the occasional interaction with an FBI agent. With the exception of the HRT guys, who were solid, most agents he'd come in contact with were dicks. It was like it was part of the FBI's employment requirement. He'd rather deal with any other agency than them.

They liked to showboat and get their names in the news for closing a big case. Finding out that Enzo De Fiore was alive and then nailing him to the wall with a lengthy prison sentence was just the type of thing that would have the Feds salivating.

Aaron didn't care about any of that shit. He didn't care if De Fiore was dead or alive. He just wanted to make sure Tegan was safe, protected.

This need to take care of her, to look out for her, had taken him off guard. Yeah, he'd been attracted to her since pretty much the day he'd met her. He couldn't deny that to himself. And after seeing the friendly, genuine way she was with customers, he'd started to simply *like* her. But now that he knew what she'd been through, he flat out respected her. Not many people could have gone on the run like she had and come out of it okay.

And stealing a gangster's dog? That just made him adore her more even if he hated that she'd put herself in danger. She'd gotten under his skin and no matter that he told himself to go slow, he wasn't sure he could take his own advice.

There was a steady hum of activity at the precinct but he was tucked down a hallway so he couldn't hear what was going on in the bullpen. Only two detectives had passed him in the hall in the last hour. So when Porter Caldwell stepped into view at the end of the hallway, he straightened, surprised.

Porter was his direct boss, though he'd taken a more hands-on role for many years with Red Stone before taking over one of the security divisions. And the guy was a former Marine, too. *Semper Fi.* Hard not to like the man.

He nodded once as Porter reached him, a small laptop bag in his hand. "Everything okay?"

"Yeah. Carlito called me. Stopped by so I could talk to your girl."

Surprise flickered through him. Tegan might not be his girl, but he wasn't going to correct Porter.

Aaron had planned to tell Porter what was going on with Tegan. When he'd called to let Porter know he was taking time off, the other man had kept things brief because he was on the way to the hospital. His sister-in-law was about to give birth—or maybe she had already—so Aaron was more than a little surprised he was here now. "What's going on with Grant and Belle?"

Porter half smiled. "False alarm but, man, she's close. And they're both ready for that kid to get here."

Aaron snorted. "They'll have their hands full soon enough. How's Maddox?"

"Keeping us busy..." He trailed off as the door to Carlito's office opened.

A man and a woman, both wearing staid dark suits and neutral expressions, stepped out. They barely glanced at Porter or Aaron as they headed down the hallway, murmuring quietly to each other.

Aaron moved into Carlito's office, wanting to make sure Tegan was okay.

Her face lit up when she saw him. His heart squeezed at the sight. Yeah, he'd definitely started to fall for her, no use denying it. For the drive here she'd tucked all her hair into a winter cap, and had worn sunglasses and adorable earmuffs to hide her ears. If whoever was after her had access to any CCTVs or facial recognition software they shouldn't be able to locate her. She'd since taken off the disguise so that her wavy auburn hair was down and around her face.

She stood and he had the strongest urge to pull her into his arms, to comfort her. So he did. He didn't give a shit what anyone else thought either. It had been so damn long since he'd felt this way about anyone. The truth was what he felt for Tegan was more than a case of lust. More than anything he'd experienced in the past. She was so easy to be around.

She leaned into his hold, burying her face against his chest. "They asked a billion questions," she muttered. "And they asked the same question ten different ways. Like they think I'm freaking stupid, or lying."

Both Carlito and Porter snorted quietly, clearly not surprised.

She pulled back and looked at Porter curiously. "I know you from somewhere. You're Lizzy's husband. She was showing off a picture of your son at the shop a while ago and you were in it."

Porter flushed, surprising Aaron. He cleared his throat. "Yeah, she said she'd met you." He looked back at Aaron. "When you told me you needed time off, I didn't realize it had to do with that bombing until Carlito called me."

Carlito leaned against the front of his desk, watching them in silence.

"If you need a safe house we'll set one up," Porter continued.

Tegan's eyes widened slightly as she looked up at Aaron, the question in her blue gaze. Did he want her to go to one?

He quickly weighed the idea. No one knew where she was, and they'd taken all precautions to keep her location quiet so that even the Feds didn't know she was with him. His son was safe and with his parents for the next few days. Since Dillon was on Christmas break he didn't have to worry about school either. Bottom line, if Tegan went to a safe house, she'd be away from him.

Nope, not happening.

He looked at Porter. "She's good with me. If that changes, I'll let you know."

Porter nodded once, as if he'd expected the answer. "I'd like to set up extra security. Something subtle. One agent in front of your place keeping an eye on things."

Yeah, Aaron had thought of the same thing. "I'll pay—"

Porter cut him off with a shake of his head. "This is pro bono. Call it a Christmas present. Anyone could have been hurt in that bombing. Her car was outside a children's boutique." Porter's jaw tightened, rage bleeding into his eyes as he took a breath. "We want to help."

"We?" Tegan asked.

"Me, my brothers—Red Stone. We won't tolerate this kind of shit in our city."

Tegan blinked once but Aaron wasn't surprised. The owners of Red Stone were civic-minded, but if Porter thought Aaron considered Tegan his, then his boss would go out of his way to keep her safe.

Porter held out the laptop bag to Tegan. "This is for you. Carlito said you'd be taking time off work at the coffee shop but would be working on your design business. My wife told me that this laptop is heavily encrypted so if anyone tries to track your movements online, you'll be safe."

Aaron had been with Red Stone Security for five years and, while he'd always been happy with his job and knew the guys he worked with were good men, this went above and beyond anything he'd expected. He'd have never asked for this kind of assistance. Hell, he hadn't even thought about her laptop.

Tegan looked at Porter, wide-eyed, her surprised expression adorable. She seemed to be shocked that anyone was helping her at all, let alone for free.

"Thank you," she finally murmured, looking unsure as she took it.

Porter cleared his throat, flicked a glance at Carlito, and said, "We're looking into De Fiore, too."

Carlito sighed and pushed up from the desk. "Yeah, I'm not hearing this. I'm gonna grab some coffee. I'll be back in a few minutes."

Tegan frowned as the detective closed the door behind him. "What just happened?"

Aaron wrapped an arm around her shoulders and pulled her close. "Carlito doesn't want to hear what we're talking about. Porter has no business looking into De Fiore but Lizzy is...good with computers."

Tegan frowned slightly. "Oh. Okay. So she's researching him?"

"Not exactly." Porter's voice was dry. "More like she's hunting him. If he's alive, there's a good chance she'll find him. Just depends on how far underground he is."

Now Tegan's eyes widened. "You mean she's, like, a hacker?"

Porter didn't answer one way or another but his expression was enough.

"Okay, wow. I...can see that." Tegan's lips curved into a grin. "I started talking code to her about one of the websites I was redesigning and she totally geeked out. She's one of the few people to ever understand me."

Porter just snorted. "If there's anything you think might be pertinent about De Fiore, anything you know, send it to her."

"Ah, I will, but I really don't know much about him. Other than he's a monster who threatened to kill me and maybe tried to kill me yesterday. Also, I don't know how to contact Lizzy."

"I've got her info," Aaron murmured.

"Good, then. I'm heading out." Porter looked between the two of them. "I don't know that I'll even be there if my sister-in-law goes into labor, but either way, bring Tegan to the Christmas party Friday if you guys are going stir crazy. My condo's one of the safest places in the city. We'll arrange a secure pickup so you don't drive your own vehicle and there's no possibility of either of you being seen inside or caught on a CCTV."

"I will." Aaron shook his hand, grateful to have such a good boss. He turned to Tegan as Porter left. "Red Stone has a lot of parties over the holidays. They're having one at Porter's place for the security teams directly under him. It's fun and he's right. His place is locked down tight and if we take the right precautions it'll be okay to take you."

Her brow furrowed slightly. "Don't feel like you have to take me. I'm just grateful you're giving me a place to lie low and that you've helped me with all this. If I go stir crazy it's a small price to pay for safety."

"I *want* to take you." And yeah, he was caveman enough to admit that he'd take pleasure in showing her off. If he thought the place wasn't secure, he'd never consider it but...taking Tegan to a Christmas party with his coworkers and friends? She was the kind of woman he wanted to bring with him. Sure, she was beautiful, but it was more than that. She was fun to be around and wouldn't freak out on him if he left her alone for a few minutes. She had no problem making conversation with other people. Unlike his ex—and he hated that he was even comparing the two of them. There was no comparison. Tegan was one of a kind.

"Yeah?"

"Yes. I would be proud to."

Her cheeks flushed an adorable shade of crimson. With her auburn hair and pale skin, it was impossible for her to hide her reactions, and he loved that he could read her so easily right now.

"We'll see how things go."

He could understand her cautiousness, but that didn't mean he had to like it. And at least it wasn't a no. His gaze dropped to her mouth and all his muscles pulled taut as he ordered his body under control. He was thirty-fucking-one, he'd been in control of his body a long damn time. Except around Tegan apparently. "Just we'll see?" he murmured.

Her eyes went heavy-lidded and whether she was aware of it or not, she leaned into him just a fraction. She inhaled slightly, as if she was smelling him. "I'm still trying to come to terms with this sweeter version of Aaron Fitzpatrick, rather than the man who used to growl at me every time I saw him."

"I never growled."

"Hmm."

"I'm a big teddy bear." He kept his voice low as he slowly reached for her, grasping one of her hips in a purely possessive hold.

When her lips curved up, he groaned. Her mouth had starred in all his fantasies in the past eight months. Every. Single. One. She'd consumed all his thoughts to the point of distraction.

Her bottom lip was just a little fuller so she looked as if she was always pouting. What he wouldn't give to—

The door opened and Carlito stepped in. He looked between them, his expression apologetic. "I've got a couple leads I need to follow up on De Fiore. I'm heading out."

And that was their cue to leave as well. Disappointment washed over Aaron that the kiss was interrupted, but he shelved it.

Sooner or later he was going to finally get a taste of Tegan. Once he did, he was pretty sure he wasn't letting her go.

* * *

Moving carefully, Alec scaled the fence to Tegan's backyard and jumped down. The yard was small and lined up perfectly with all the others on the street. He'd just called in multiple bomb threats to a school very close by, giving specific details of where the bombs were located and what he'd used to make them. The details— and the similarity to the bomb he'd used on Tegan O'Kelly's car—were too much for the cops to ignore.

The city was on alert after the car bombing so he knew that her security detail would be called off her house, at least temporarily.

Which was all he needed so he could get inside and kill her. If she was even there. And Alec wasn't sure she was. He'd been by her place of work and he'd heard her boss mention something to another employee about Tegan being away indefinitely.

It was twilight so he used the cover of falling darkness to make quick work of jimmying her sliding glass door open. The security here was shockingly pathetic. Inside he immediately saw the motion sensor so he paused where he was and listened.

It was quiet. The kind of quiet that told him he was alone. There was no dog to greet or attack him, and he knew she had a dog. Still, he had to be certain she wasn't here. Because he wasn't passing up an opportunity to kill her if she was.

Alec lay down on his belly. He was familiar with most security systems, and sensors were usually programed to ignore anything under two or three feet if the owner had a pet. Belly crawling, he made his way down a hallway until he reached the foyer.

When he stood in front of the keypad, the alarm started beeping so he popped the cover off and placed the device on it he'd used many times before. Less than ten seconds later, the beeping stopped.

If you're here, you're dead.

It wasn't personal, something he doubted she'd understand. Pulling out his weapon, he made his way upstairs. Considering no one had come to investigate the alarm going off he was almost positive he didn't need his gun, but being prepared had saved his ass on more than one occasion. It was why he was always armed and, more often than not, wore gloves. No need to leave behind any trace of himself.

He swept the entire upstairs then focused on her bedroom. No laptop, and it was clear some clothes were missing from her closet. Not many, but enough empty hangers indicated she might have packed a bag.

After he finished checking the rest of the house, he saw that her dishwasher was empty, there were no dirty dishes in the sink, and the sink was completely dry, as if it hadn't been used in at least a day. And her heat had been turned off.

His gut told him she was hiding out somewhere. He just hoped she hadn't gone on the run again. Looking around her place, he didn't think she had. There were too many things she owned still here, things she wouldn't leave behind.

In her small office he riffled through what few files she had. Like most people she would pay whatever bills she had online anyway. Still, he needed a clue to where the hell she was.

When he found nothing, he headed out the way he'd come and set the alarm to away mode so it would arm itself. He made sure there was no trace that he'd ever been there.

Though he was frustrated, he kept his annoyance in check. He was a professional and used to setbacks. Hunting people took time. For years he'd done freelance work, just killing for hire. Now he had a boss and, though Alec knew he'd be angry that she wasn't dead yet, the man would just have to deal with it. In his opinion, his boss should have killed her long ago.

But De Fiore hadn't shown an interest in hunting her after he'd 'died.' Not at first anyway. A couple of weeks ago, De Fiore had made contact with Alec, of all people, and told him he might need help with getting a new false ID once he killed the O'Kelly woman. De Fiore hadn't been sure how things would play out here in Miami and wanted a backup ID in case the one he already had in place somehow got flagged.

Alec was simply going to flush pretty Tegan O'Kelly out if he couldn't find her. Make the bitch come to him. Sometimes that was the only way to do things, to make your prey come to you. He couldn't risk De Fiore getting to her first.

Once Alec was in the safety of his newly stolen car, he turned on the voice digitizer app and called her cell phone.

No surprise, it went directly to voice mail. "If you make me hunt you down any longer I'm going to start killing your friends. I'll start with your whore boss and her son. I'll record their deaths so you can watch them both beg and scream. I'll do the kid first." He ended the call and tossed the phone out the window. The phone was a burner but he wouldn't be using it anymore in case the cops tried to track him.

He wasn't actually going to kill a kid—he did have some scruples after all—but he knew the message would freak her out. It might make her scared enough to get sloppy.

He didn't think the message would make her come out of hiding. Not yet anyway. He was going to leave more messages and make each one worse than the last.

The messages would put her on edge and guarantee she'd call her friends to check on them. From the little he'd watched Tegan he knew she was close with the woman who owned the bakery. A few more messages like that and Tegan O'Kelly would be compelled to call her friends. Once she did, he'd be able to get a location on her—because he was watching her boss's cell phone, waiting for any call from Tegan. Soon enough he'd get a lock on her location. From there, he'd track her down and put a bullet in her head.

CHAPTER SEVEN

Aaron stopped outside the entryway to his living room and eavesdropped on Tegan and Dillon. It had been almost two days since she'd talked to the Feds and so far neither they nor the Miami PD had been able to locate De Fiore. If he was even *in* Miami. Aaron knew they were exploring all leads on the bomber and so far all the cops had been able to find was a few images of a man in a hoodie heading down the street where the bomb had been placed.

They had a time frame for when they thought it had been planted. It had been early in the morning and the man's image had been caught on multiple CCTVs. But the guy had disappeared into the parking garage of a hotel and from there they hadn't been able to trace him anywhere. Without an actual face or fingerprints, they were hunting a ghost. It could be De Fiore or not.

"You don't have to let me win, you know," Dillon said.

"I'm not. I just stink at this game." Tegan's voice was matter of fact.

Dillon giggled, the sound music to Aaron's ears. He might have screwed up by marrying the wrong woman, but he'd gotten Dillon so it was worth it.

"You really are bad. Not as bad as Daddy. We can play something else if you want."

"It's okay, it's still fun. So your dad stinks, too?"

Dillon gave a belly laugh. "He can't even get past level two."

Tegan laughed loudly and Aaron risked peeking around the entryway. The Christmas tree twinkled in the corner, brightening the room. The two of them were sitting on the ground in front of the television, their backs to him. Kali was snoozing next to Tegan, her body stretched out as she lightly snored. Dillon was wearing his Captain America pajamas and Tegan had on a black party dress with a big puffy skirt that had sparkles all over it. It puffed out around her on the ground. Her hair was pulled up in a twist, revealing the smooth, pale skin of her neck and back.

He'd never really thought of backs as sexy, but everything about Tegan was.

Unfortunately, they hadn't had much time alone together since the meeting in Carlito's office. She'd been working on her website designs for the past day and a half, and he was pretty certain she'd been keeping him at a healthy distance after their almost-kiss. Much to his annoyance. He was patient, though. And determined.

"So...are you my dad's girlfriend now?"

Tegan's entire body jolted and he watched as the character on her side of the screen fell off a cliff. She cleared her throat. "Ah, no. We're just friends."

Unfortunately, he thought. He planned to change that soon, though.

"Yeah, that's what he said. I just thought maybe...you guys might not wanna tell me."

"I don't think your dad would ever lie to you."

"I know. But I heard Nana talking to Grandpa about you when they thought I was asleep. She said you were lovely and that it was about time Daddy moved on. I don't really know what she means but I know she likes you. I thought maybe you might be my new mommy."

Aaron winced. Tegan was silent for a long moment and he wasn't sure if he should interrupt the conversation or just let it play out. Dillon had asked about 'getting a new mommy' a couple of times in the last few months so this wasn't exactly out of the blue. He'd even put *mommy* on his Christmas list for Santa. Aaron hated that his son had missed out on a solid, loving, maternal presence.

"I like your dad but we really are just friends. He's helping me out right now by letting me stay here. So how about I be your friend, too?"

"I'd like that. You know, Nana lets me have ice cream whenever I want. Now that we're friends, maybe you can give me ice cream when I want, too."

Tegan snorted. "Your Nana lets you get away with a lot. And the answer is no. You're already killing me in this game. I can't reward that."

"So if I let you win, you'll give me ice cream?"

Tegan barked out a laugh. "No, but nice try."

Aaron quickly moved out of sight as the doorbell chimed. He waited a few beats then stepped into the foyer and in full view of the living room.

"Nana!" Dillon flew past him, moving at light speed before Aaron reached the door.

"Wait." Aaron hurried to the door and looked through the peephole before opening it. He'd tried to explain to Dillon why they had to be extra careful right now but, at five, he just didn't understand the concept of real danger. He barely understood 'stranger danger.'

Aaron pulled open the door and smiled when he saw his mom and dad bundled up in their winter coats. They were earlier than they needed to be, which...was nice. He wondered if his mom had planned that. The Red Stone driver wouldn't be here for another hour. Which would give him much wanted alone time with Tegan.

Dillon jumped into his dad's arms as Aaron hugged his mom. "Thanks for keeping him tonight." They'd agreed to take him so he and Tegan could attend the Christmas party.

Part of him didn't want to go—he'd rather stay here with no one but Tegan for company—but he figured she could use some time away from her voluntary lock-down. She was so positive about everything, never complaining. He wanted to give this to her.

"We should be thanking you," his mom said, kissing him on the cheek. Her gaze strayed past him to Tegan, who he heard entering the foyer. "You look stunning, dear."

"Thank you," she murmured.

Aaron turned around and got the full view of her—and forgot to breathe. He'd only seen her back so far but this...

Her blue eyes seemed bigger, brighter tonight. Her makeup was darker, smoky, and he realized her dress was a dark blue, not black. It shimmered when she moved toward him. She had an almost hesitant smile on her face.

He tried not to stare, but he swept his gaze over her, taking in everything. Her heels were strappy, lacing around her ankles and sexy as fuck. He imagined her wearing nothing but them, digging the spikes into his back as he buried his face between her legs. And the pain would be worth it to taste her, pleasure her. All the tension from the last couple of days coiled tight in his belly as he watched her. He was so damn hungry for her. He was vaguely aware of the others talking but he just stared at Tegan until he felt a sharp nudge against his rib cage from his mom.

"You look beautiful," he rasped out, knowing he needed to say something.

Tegan smiled, her shoulders seeming to lose their tension at his words. As if she could doubt how incredible she was. She was a goddess.

"Well, we're going to get out of your hair," his mother said, already snapping the leash onto Kali's collar. "I don't want you to be late."

Oh yeah, she'd definitely come early for a reason. Aaron could hear it in the tone of her voice.

"And it's hot cocoa time!" Dillon was jumping up and down by the open front door as his dad helped Dillon into his jacket.

Aaron smiled at his son's excitement. "I'll have my phone on me and—"

"I know all that," his mom said, waving a hand in the air. "We've done this a thousand times. We're watching a Christmas movie tonight and having popcorn and hot cocoa. We'll be fine. I'll see you in the morning."

He knew they would be okay, but it was still habit to go over everything with them.

Once Dillon had hugged both him and Tegan and they were gone, he shut the door behind them, glad to be alone with her. Guilt slid through him because he loved his son more than anything, but he craved some alone time with Tegan. Desperately.

If he had anything to say about it, the walls she'd put up between them were coming down tonight. "You really are beautiful." The words came out raspier than before. He couldn't stop staring at her, wanting her. He tried to shove back his impatience that things between them were moving so slow.

Her cheeks flushed pink. "You said cocktail party-type dress so...I thought this would work."

It worked all right. Too well.

He took a step closer to her, wanting to touch her. They'd almost kissed in Carlito's office and it was all he'd been able to think about the past two days. He'd been trying to keep himself on lockdown for her because it had been clear she was keeping a stupid wall between them. For so damn long it had felt as if he was existing in a haze. He'd been living a celibate existence that would have been foreign to him before five years ago. Now all his control and patience were on a wire's edge. "I want to kiss you right now."

Her eyes widened at his blunt statement. "Aaron, you can't...just say that."

"Yes I can." He covered the rest of the short distance between them, his shoes quiet against the wood floor. He didn't reach out and touch her even though his entire body ached with the need to do just that. "I want to taste all of you. Shove that pretty dress up to your waist and bury my face between your legs. I want to make you come so hard you can barely walk afterward."

Her eyes grew even wider, her breathing shaky and erratic as she stared at him, her mouth parting just a fraction. There was a slight gloss to her pink lips.

"Nothing to say to that?" he murmured. His libido revved to life whenever he was around her. He wanted nothing more than to devour Tegan. He wasn't holding back anything now. He'd realized that by playing it passive, by not being more direct with her, he was cheating them both out of something that could be amazing. He knew he could get burned by her, but he was done with living like a monk. She'd woken something up inside him and he wasn't going to run from it. She made him feel alive again in the most primal way.

Her eyes were dilated as she swallowed hard, watching him with a mix of emotions. One of them was fear. He knew she wasn't afraid of him so maybe it was just what was between them.

"Just think about my words all night while we're at the party. It's what I'm going to be thinking about doing to you. What I think about all the damn time—what I thought about this morning while I jerked off in the shower." He knew he was pushing her and didn't care. Those walls had to come down.

Her cheeks were bright crimson now. "Aaron…"

A groan tore from him. "I love it when you say my name." He'd imagined her saying it under very different circumstances.

A shudder racked her and she took a step forward. She lifted a hand as if to touch him, but dropped it just as quickly. "I'm not ready for...a relationship. So much is going on and you're a dad and...I just, I don't think it would work."

Every single thing she said was an excuse. "Do you want me?"

She blinked those pretty blue eyes. "Yes, of course."

The way she said *of course*, as if the need was a given, made his cock even harder. "Then that's all that matters. If you want to keep things between us casual, whatever happens can be just between us." Complete and utter bullshit, but he was going to get through her barriers. Whatever she seemed to think wouldn't work between them, he'd just tear up all her excuses one day at a time until there was nothing keeping them apart. If that meant keeping things between them quiet, that was okay. For now.

She bit her bottom lip. "Really?" The word was a whisper. He could see that she wanted to kiss him, that he was breaking through her defenses.

He advanced on her and she took a step back. He kept moving until her back was against the wall by the staircase and he was pressed against her from chest to groin.

Her breathing was erratic as she looked up at him. His cock pressed hard against her abdomen. There was no way she could doubt he wanted her.

When she placed tentative hands on his chest, he slowly lowered his head, giving her enough time to tell him to stop. If she didn't, absolutely nothing was going to interrupt them this time.

Her eyes started to close and she leaned up to meet him. She let out a little sigh of pleasure as their lips finally touched.

Even though he wanted to slide his fingers through her thick hair, the twist looked complicated and he didn't want to mess it up. He gently gripped the side of her neck and part of her jaw so that he could feel her pulse point.

It was going crazy.

She moaned into his mouth as he kissed her and nipped at his bottom lip. He loved the feel of her tongue and sweet kisses. He wasn't sure how long he lost himself in tasting her, their mouths and tongues teasing each other.

When she arched into him, rubbing against him with her whole body, he pulled back just a fraction so he could kiss a path along her jaw and neck. She sucked in a breath when he reached the juncture of her neck and shoulder.

His control was close to breaking, his cock rock hard, but right now was about her. He wanted to worship her entire body, to spend hours learning all her curves. For now, he was going to taste her as she came against his face. He was going to get her addicted to him and he wanted to stake a claim on her sweet body. She'd be thinking about him all night after this, about how he'd made her feel.

Her hands slid through his short hair, her fingers gripping him as he bent down in front of her. He looked up the length of her body to see her staring down at him, her blue eyes bright with hunger.

Keeping his gaze locked on hers, he reached under the puffy skirt of her dress, his hands skimming up the outside of her smooth thighs until he reached the silky material of her panties. Oh so slowly, he tugged them down her legs, his heart pounded wildly.

Her breath caught in her throat as she stepped out of them. But she spread her legs apart just a little wider, the invitation clear.

This was hotter, more intense than he'd fantasized about. The skirt of her dress had too much material to shove up to her waist and stay in place, so he ducked his head under it. This was sexier anyway. Not being able to see her while he pleasured her, just hearing her moans. He wondered if she'd be loud or restrained. Either choice was a good one but he wanted to hear her go crazy and let go.

She let out a yelp of surprise as he moved between her legs and lifted one over his shoulder, draping it across his back and giving him all the access he needed.

The dim light of the foyer filtered through enough that he could see her sweet pussy. She was completely bare—shaved or waxed, he couldn't tell. Didn't matter. The sight made him groan. Before he tasted her, he dipped a finger between her folds.

She was soaked. The knowledge that she was turned on because of him sent another rush of heat spiraling through him.

Whatever excuses she came up with as for why now wasn't the right time for a relationship, she couldn't deny the chemistry they had together. That would have been impossible to do and be believable. He'd been fighting it from the moment he met the feisty woman.

Her hips rolled as he slid his finger deeper inside her. It was strange not being able to see her face, but incredibly sexy to be solely focused on her pussy and have her literally trembling as she waited to feel what he'd do.

"Aaron." She moaned out his name, as if begging him to do more.

He would gladly oblige. Burying his face between her legs, he flicked his tongue up the length of her wet folds. She groaned, her hips bucking against him as he teased her.

Her taste and scent were sweet perfection against his tongue. Almost as sweet as the little sounds of pleasure she was making. He was surprised by how loud she was, her pleas for him to do more making his cock even harder, something he hadn't thought possible.

"My clit, my clit," she moaned out, the words half begging, half demand.

The demand nearly pushed him over the edge. He hadn't expected that of her, but he probably should have. He'd been intent on teasing her longer, dragging this out, but he was driven with the need to make her come. To taste it. Knowing she was right on the precipice because of him. All the muscles in his body pulled tight, his focus purely on making her come.

Shifting his head slightly, he zeroed in on the little bundle of nerves peeking out from her folds. Her clit was already swollen and just begging for his touch. He rubbed his tongue over it as he slid a finger fully inside her. She was so tight, her inner walls clenching around him as he began stroking her clit.

Her hips moved in rhythm with his tongue, her moans louder and louder, telling him that he was playing her body right. She was absolute perfection.

He added another finger, buried them both deep. She jerked hard, dug her heeled shoe into his back as her inner walls clenched harder around his fingers.

"Oh...Aaron..." Her climax hit, and her body writhed against him as she came.

He continued stroking her clit, not letting up the pressure until she begged him to stop. He swiped his tongue against her one last time before ducking back out from under her skirt.

His entire body trembled with the need to fill her, his cock pressing insistently against his zipper. This had been about her, though.

Her eyes were heavy-lidded as she looked down at him, her breathing erratic and an expression of pure satisfaction on her face. After pressing soft kisses to her inner ankle and thigh, he reached back, gently wrapped his fingers around her ankle, and brought her foot off his back.

When he set her foot on the ground, he wanted nothing more than to strip her dress off completely and bury himself inside her. But he was pretty sure it was too soon for that. Not for him, but he didn't want to push her too fast. Not when he knew she was hesitant to commit to anything. He wanted her to come to him, to have no regrets about them. Because once they crossed that line, he wouldn't let her go. Not without a fight.

She grabbed his shoulders and tugged on him. He obeyed her silent command and stood, his legs shaking. To his surprise, she started unbuckling his pants.

He groaned, letting her take over. Grasping the back of her head, he slid his fingers through her hair. He didn't give a fuck if it got messed up now. He wanted to stamp himself on all of her, so that when she looked in the mirror she saw him there, imprinted on her in the subtlest of ways.

"Fuck, Tegan," he rasped out as she shoved his pants and boxers down.

Her elegant fingers wrapped around his hard length, gripping him at the base. He rocked into her hold, crushing his mouth against hers as she started stroking him. God, it had been so damn long, and knowing it was Tegan touching him...

She pumped him hard, making him lose any train of thought so that all he could do was feel that soft hand bringing him the sweetest pleasure.

His balls pulled up tight as his climax started to build. He wished he was inside her, that her tight sheath was wrapped around him as he came. That would come soon enough, though.

The base of his spine tingled, his orgasm so damn close. Though he hated to pull away from her, at the last minute he pulled back and took over, coming all over his shirt and stomach instead of her dress. She might not care but she looked so fucking gorgeous, and even though he wanted to mark her, he held back. Next time he'd come in her or on her stomach, mark her with himself. Yeah, it was a fucking primitive thought, but she apparently brought out that side of him.

Hunger glittered in her gaze as she watched him, drinking in the sight of him as he finished himself off. Her lips were parted slightly, glossy from their kiss.

As the last of his orgasm ripped through him, he threw his head back, groaning her name. When he opened his eyes, she was still watching him. She looked so damn sexy and just a little vulnerable standing there with wisps of hair tumbling around her face, her lips swollen.

"You're the sexiest woman I've ever fucking met," he rasped out, hating that his words didn't come close to how he felt about her.

She smiled, though, and half her mouth pulled up in a sweet, sensual movement that he felt to his core.

"I didn't let you finish because I didn't want to mess up your dress. Next time though..." He let the words hang in the air, letting her fill in whatever blanks she wanted.

"Next time?" she whispered.

"There will be a next time."

At that she smiled, and something inside him loosened that he hadn't even realized was coiled tight.

He leaned down and brushed his lips across hers, needing to taste her again. "I've gotta get cleaned up," he murmured, hating to pull away from her.

Looking a little dazed, she lifted a hand to her hair and half laughed. "I think I probably need to as well."

After a long moment, she pushed away from the wall, her cheeks still pink as she made her way to the stairs.

He wanted to forget the party and just stay there with her, to take her to bed and spend hours pleasuring each other. But their driver would arrive soon.

And he could be patient. He was pretty sure he'd pushed her enough for right now. At the party he planned to flirt with her, tease her until she couldn't stand it. Then he'd make his move. Afterward he hoped they ended up very naked together. The first time of many to come.

CHAPTER EIGHT

Tegan stepped into Aaron's house and immediately disarmed the security system as Kali raced for the kitchen to get to her food and water bowl. She knew Aaron and Dillon wouldn't be there but a thread of disappointment still wound its way through her that they were gone. She'd thought last night would turn out very differently, that she would get to spend a lot of naked time with Aaron after the party.

But on the way there they'd gotten a call from Bree that Dillon had thrown up so they'd headed back and picked him up. The poor little guy had been puking all night so she'd slept in the living room on the opposite couch to Aaron and Dillon.

Aaron had told her that she hadn't needed to stay with them, but she'd really wanted to. Seeing Dillon's face so pale had scared her. Aaron had taken everything in stride, though, handling it like a boss. The man was amazing to her. She'd been internally panicking, but Aaron had dealt with it so steadily, like he seemed to do everything. Even though Dillon's fever was down and he'd stopped throwing up, Aaron had taken him to a walk-in clinic this morning.

She'd wanted to go, especially since Dillon had asked her to, but it wasn't a possibility. So far no one knew about her connection to Aaron and she wasn't going to make them targets by potentially being seen with them in public. Last night they'd taken protective measures with a driver and an armored vehicle that no one could possibly see inside so she wouldn't be caught on any CCTVs or traffic cameras. It wouldn't be as easy today and it wasn't worth risking. Nothing was worth risking Aaron or Dillon's safety.

After hanging up her coat, scarf, and hat—all of which doubled as her camouflage while out walking her dog—she hooked Kali's leash next to her stuff. Holding onto her gloves, she followed after Kali, who'd collapsed in a heap by her food and water bowls, apparently exhausted from their long walk.

Since Tegan wasn't using her cell phone, she picked up Aaron's landline. It was a little weird using an actual landline since she hadn't in years.

"Hey, you," Kimmy said, picking up on the second ring. She was one of the very few people who knew where Tegan was staying.

"Hey, yourself. How's everything going?"

Kimmy gave a short laugh. "I think I should be asking you that."

"Ah, well enough." Her face heated up as she thought about what she and Aaron had done the night before, how he'd gone down on her right up against the wall— how she'd begged him. Her nipples pebbled just thinking about it. "It's weird being disconnected from everything and not being able to go home. But it is what it is." Eight months ago she would have been used to being disconnected. Now, after settling into a new life, she'd gotten used to being able to call friends when she wanted and do things when she wanted. Not look over her shoulder like a hunted fugitive. It infuriated her that someone had forced her to change all that again.

"I'm sure you're going to have a ton of voice mails. Everyone's been asking about you at the shop."

She inwardly cringed. Crap. She'd been checking her e-mail and staying up to date with her design projects the last few days but she hadn't checked her voice mail since everything happened. *Crap, crap, crap.* She'd been in contact with her insurance company about her car and had given them Aaron's home phone number to contact instead of her cell. "How's everyone else doing? Are all the shops open?"

"Things are kinda tense down here, but all the shops are open and, surprisingly, we're all doing incredible business. I guess people are just morbid or something and want to see where the bomb went off because we're getting a lot of new business. Cops have been down here, too, more than once, questioning and re-questioning everyone."

"I just hope they find whoever did it." A shiver racked through her, chills dotting her arms and the back of her neck. The longer it took for the police or FBI to find any leads, the harder it was for her to stay positive.

"No kidding. Let me know if you need anything. I haven't told anyone where you are. Most people are just glad you're okay but some of the shop owners are freaking nosy." She snorted. "Old Mr. Pritchett was insistent he know where you are. It was ridiculous. I told him if the cops thought he should know, they'd tell him."

Tegan laughed, not at all surprised. Mr. Pritchett ran the hardware store and was grumpy twenty-four-seven. It was his only setting. And not grumpy like Aaron used to be. Mr. Pritchett was a fussy old man who gossiped more than anyone she'd ever met. "I'm just glad everyone's okay and that the businesses weren't affected."

"Me, too."

They talked for a few minutes and once they disconnected she used Aaron's phone to call her voice mail. Kali whined at the back door as she started listening. Twenty-two new messages. Not as bad as she'd expected but still, yikes.

She opened the back door, letting her dog out as she started listening to her voice mail. Leaning against the doorframe, she watched Kali race around the yard. When she got to the tenth message her blood iced over as a digital voice came across the line.

"If you make me hunt you down any longer I'm going to start killing your friends. I'll start with your whore boss and her son. I'll record their deaths so you can watch them both beg and scream. I'll do the kid first."

Her fingers were numb as the call ended. Fumbling, she saved the message then disconnected.

She called Kimmy back, her heart pounding erratically in her chest. *Pick up, pick up—*

"Hey—"

"Where's Brendan? Is he okay?"

"He's fine. He's here today, actually. What's going on?" Kimmy's voice went from calm to worried in a second.

"I just got a creepy message from someone saying they're going to hurt you and Brendan. Their voice was disguised so I don't know who it was, but it could have been the person who planted the bomb." She hated even saying the words out loud. She almost felt as if once she did it would give credence to them, to put the reality out there in the universe.

Kimmy sucked in a sharp breath.

"Is Callan with you?"

"Yeah, he's been helping out all week. He and Brendan are in the back making cookies."

Some of the tension around Tegan's chest eased, but not by much. She needed them to be safe, not out in public for some lunatic to attack. "Okay, good. I'm going to call the detective on the case and tell him about this. I just wanted to make sure you were okay. Are you going to get Brendan out of there?"

"Yeah. Jeez, this is crazy." She let out a shaky sigh. "I'm going to close the shop right now and get out of here." Kimmy's voice was trembling and Tegan couldn't blame her.

The bomb was terrifying enough but this direct threat against people she cared for was worse. She kept playing those words over and over in her head. "Good. I'll call you in an hour." After she got out of there and to a safe house. She had to get away, for Aaron and Dillon's sake. "I've got to call the cops and let them know about this." For all she knew they'd be able to track where the call to her phone had come from. She also needed to call Porter Caldwell and see if he'd been serious about that safe house offer because she wasn't staying there a moment longer.

She knew Aaron would try to convince her to stay but it wasn't happening. Whoever had left that message had no problem threatening kids. So far very few people knew where she was staying or her link to Aaron. She planned to keep it that way.

Getting far away from him as soon as possible was her only option.

* * *

Tegan's hands trembled as she pulled out a suitcase from her closet. "You don't have to stay here while I pack." If anything, the uniformed police officer's presence made her even shakier. It was a reminder that she was in danger, that her house wasn't safe right now. This was the place she'd made her own, where she'd added her personal touches, where she'd felt freaking safe when she put her head on her pillow at night. She wondered if she'd ever feel safe again.

After calling Detective Duarte, he'd sent over the uniformed officer who'd been watching her place to pick her up since he'd been the closest to Aaron's home. She'd been ready to call a cab, anything to get away from Aaron's place as fast as possible.

Being there had felt like she was contaminating his home, making him *and* Dillon targets. Aaron was going to be upset that she'd left, but she hadn't been willing to wait. She wasn't sure how long he'd be at the clinic anyway.

The officer nodded politely. "I'll be downstairs if you need me." He was about six feet tall with dark hair and dark eyes, and his solid presence reminded her of Aaron. Which just made her feel crappier.

Before the man had taken two steps back toward her bedroom door, the doorbell rang. "Stay put," he ordered. The officer tensed and placed his hand on the butt of his secured weapon. He didn't draw it, but he hurried out the door and down the stairs.

She figured it was a neighbor or possibly a reporter but still tensed as she followed after him. She stayed at the top of the stairs, mostly following his orders. It wouldn't be Carlito yet—he'd told her that he was in Coconut Grove following up on an anonymous tip about an Enzo De Fiore sighting. He said it sounded legit so she was hopeful he'd find the bastard.

Knock, knock, knock. "Tegan? I saw you drive up with the police. Is everything okay?" a muted female voice called.

Tension easing from her shoulders, Tegan hurried down the stairs as the officer turned to her, a question in his gaze.

"I know her. Name's Gina. She's a neighbor and a regular at my part-time job." The woman came in every day to get donuts or crepes or some sort of high-carb snack—and never seemed to put on an ounce. She must live at the gym. Or maybe just had ridiculous genes.

The officer nodded after looking through the peep-hole again and then opened the door.

"Oh…" Gina stepped back, her smile faltering as she came face-to-face with the officer, even though she had to know there was a cop there. His vehicle was in the driveway. Kinda hard to miss.

He seemed speechless, too, but more likely because of her Jessica Rabbit curves.

Gina flicked a glance over at Tegan, who was a few feet behind him. "I just wanted to stop by and see you. I brought homemade cookies." She held them up tentatively and gave a megawatt smile to the officer—who blinked, almost in a daze as he stared at her.

Right about now talking to people and making polite conversation where she pretended to be okay was the last thing Tegan wanted to do, but Gina had been up at the hospital after the bombing. They weren't exactly friends, but she lived a few doors down and always came into Kimmy's place. Tegan would feel like the biggest jerk if she turned her away. "Ah, I'm not going to be here for long, but come in for a few minutes. I appreciate you stopping by."

"Oh, I won't stay long. I just saw you get out of the police car and wanted to come over and make sure you were okay. It's good timing, too. I just finished this batch of cookies."

Tegan smiled, stepping forward as Gina entered. "We'll be fine. I'm just going to finish up packing," she said to the officer.

"Packing?" Gina popped off the lid to the white chocolate chip macadamia nut cookies. "They're fresh," she murmured to the officer. "Want one?"

He nodded, taking one. "Thank you."

"So, packing?" Gina asked again, falling in step with Tegan, who just wanted to get the hell out of her place and to the safe house Porter said he'd have ready for her.

"Ah, yeah. Just heading out of town for a few days." Not exactly true, but after talking to Carlito, she'd called Porter. He'd been adamant that she not tell anyone where she was going—as if she would anyway. She *liked* breathing. Even telling one person where the safe house was could put them and her in danger.

"Have the police found any leads about the bombing? They've been questioning everyone in this neighborhood and down by the shop. I've been questioned *three* times." Gina sat on the edge of Tegan's bed while she returned to her closet.

It was a little weird that Gina was here, but Tegan knew this was what people did. It was human nature. They brought over food and wanted to know what was going on in situations like this. Especially since they were neighbors. Still, Tegan just wanted her gone.

"I think they have a few leads." It wasn't like she could tell her anything anyway. Carlito and the FBI had been careful not to leak any information that Enzo De Fiore might be involved. Publicly they were treating it as a potential terrorist attack, not an attack against her personally. They didn't want to tip their hand that they thought De Fiore might still be alive.

"It's so scary that something like that could happen right here in Miami."

Tegan nodded, pulling a couple of shirts off a hanger. "Yeah."

"You want a cookie? They're still warm."

"I'm okay, but thanks."

"You're sure?"

Tegan turned from her closet at the odd note in Gina's voice. She sat cross-legged on the edge of Tegan's bed, her low-cut sweater showing off an insane amount of cleavage. For the first time since Tegan had met the woman, she noticed she was wearing flat black sneakers instead of her normally spiked high heels. "Yeah, I'm not really hungry. But they look great." She tried to inject some positivity into her voice, but she was mentally exhausted and, yeah, depressed that she wouldn't be staying at Aaron's anymore.

Last night, before the party they'd never made it to, had been wonderful. *Incredible.* It had been so damn long since she'd been intimate with anyone. And Aaron wasn't just *anyone.* She trusted him, adored him, and despite her better judgment had completely fallen for him. Even as she'd told herself not to, to keep her distance, it was impossible to resist him.

Gina pressed the top back onto the cookie container and sealed them in. She sighed as she did it, making Tegan feel guilty. She could force a stupid cookie down if it would make the woman feel better.

Before she could say anything, Gina reached into her clutch purse and pulled out a small gun.

Tegan sucked in a breath and stared at the weapon. "Gina, what—"

"Shut the fuck up," Gina said quietly. "You should have eaten that damn cookie and made things a hell of a lot easier on yourself."

Her body went numb. "You poisoned the cop?"

Gina rolled her eyes and pushed to her feet. Her perfectly manicured hands looked steady as she held the gun on Tegan. "He'll wake up in an hour or two with a headache." She used the gun to motion to the door. "We're leaving now. Stay in front of me and don't try anything stupid. You do, I'll shoot you in the fucking knee."

Tegan dropped the shirt she'd been clutching and somehow made her legs obey her brain. She barely remembered moving but found herself downstairs in the foyer. The cop was slumped against the door, looking almost peaceful. A quarter of the cookie was crumbled on the shiny wood floor next to one of his open hands.

"Move him out of the way," Gina snapped.

Tegan looked back at her. Gina was still holding the gun and had it pointed right at her head. "Why are you doing this?" She was going to have to get out of this on her own. But she needed to know what she was up against.

Gina lifted a shoulder, not answering one way or another. "I'm doing it for Enzo, you stupid bitch. Stop asking questions. Now move that guy. Just roll him over so we can get out the door."

Doing as she said, Tegan grunted as she shifted the man to the side. At least he was breathing. She just hoped that Gina had been telling the truth, that the guy would wake up soon. For a brief moment she contemplated taking the cop's gun, but it was secured in a holster. By the time she unsnapped it, pulled it out, and turned, she'd already be shot in the back.

When they stepped out into the bright sunshine, Tegan had to shield her eyes. Only the cop car sat in the

driveway. Gina must have just walked from her place—
oh God. Was Enzo there right now?

More ice settled around her chest, making it hard to
breathe when she saw two little kids playing across the
street as their mom watched. Even if she wanted to
scream and make a scene, there was no way she could
risk putting anyone else in danger.

Tegan had no idea how dangerous Gina truly was—
and that probably wasn't even her real name. As Tegan
turned to see how far behind her Gina was, she inwardly
cringed.

Gina stepped up right beside her and pressed the gun
into her ribs. She was using one of Tegan's jackets to
cover it up. Must have grabbed it from the coatrack in
the foyer.

"We're just going to walk down to my place and
you're going to have a little talk with my Enzo. You'll tell
him what he wants and we'll all go our separate ways."
Her voice was a low murmur as they walked across the
little stone path that led to the sidewalk.

Tegan's instinct told her to simply stop moving, to
refuse to go any farther. But she didn't know this woman at all. She had no idea if she would hurt those kids or
just shoot Tegan and run. She knew for a fact the woman was lying to her. Tegan wouldn't be walking away
from this. There was no way they'd leave her alive once
they got what they wanted—or didn't in this case. Once
they realized she didn't have what they wanted she'd be
useless. Disposable.

As they reached the sidewalk, Aaron's familiar blue
truck pulled into the driveway.

Oh God. *No, no, no.* She hadn't even seen him driving down the road, hadn't been able to focus on anything other than Gina and the gun. There was nowhere to go, nowhere to hide from him. "Let me get rid of him. If you hurt him, you'll never get your fucking diamonds," Tegan said through gritted teeth. They would never get them anyway, at least not from Tegan. But she had no problem bluffing to save Aaron's life. She couldn't let him get hurt because of her. It wasn't an option.

The woman's dark eyes narrowed slightly but she nodded. "Do it fast," she murmured.

Aaron's truck shuddered to a halt and the big, sexy man jumped out, slamming the door before he hurried toward her, moving like a lethal predator.

A mix of concern and, yeah, anger played across his features. He flicked a glance at Gina, who was still standing incredibly close to Tegan, and nodded once in a half greeting.

"What the hell are you doing?" he snapped, clearly not caring that they had an audience. He clutched a piece of paper in his hand and she realized it was the note she'd left him.

Bone-numbing fear punched through her. Why the hell had he come? "I...can't stay with you anymore. What we had was nice but I'm not interested in playing mom for your kid." The words were harsh but it was the only thing she could think of to get him to leave. "Don't call me again." She also hoped he realized that she was in danger and called the cops. Regardless, she just needed him to let her *go.* All it would take for Gina to hurt him was to raise that gun and pull the trigger.

A wave of nausea swept through her at the thought. She couldn't let that happen.

"Tegan—"

"Leave me alone!" Heat infused her words before she looked at Gina. "Come on. Let's go."

He stared at her wide-eyed, as if she'd slapped him in the face. As if he had no idea who she truly was.

He had to know better. God, she hoped so.

The whole scene was weird with the cop car in the driveway next to Aaron's truck—with no police escort in sight—and she silently prayed that Aaron realized that.

Gina tightened her fingers around Tegan's arm, hidden by the bulky jacket. The gun stayed pressed against her ribs as they started walking down the sidewalk. Once they reached the corner it wouldn't be long until they reached Gina's place. She couldn't believe Enzo had been so close to her all this time. She'd never been safe. Not truly.

Tegan's legs were stiff as she walked. She resisted the urge to turn around, to look at Aaron. She couldn't risk—

Gina grunted as a huge blur of motion slammed into her from behind.

Aaron tackled Gina, moving like a pro football player as he knocked her to the ground. The gun clattered to the sidewalk.

Without thinking, Tegan lunged for it, grabbing it as Gina screamed out in rage. The sound cut off sharply as Aaron wrenched her arms behind her back.

Gina started whimpering in pain. "Please don't hurt me. He made me do it." Her voice was so different from the demanding, angry woman she'd been inside Tegan's house.

"Shut the fuck up," Aaron snarled.

Tegan held the gun at her side, unsure if she should train it on Gina, she was shaking so badly. It was clear Aaron had everything under control as he secured her wrists together with his huge hands.

"Are you okay?" he asked, looking up at her, fear etched into every line of his face.

She nodded. "Fine." She wasn't fine, but now wasn't the time to have a breakdown. Out of the corner of her eye she saw the woman across the street rushing her kids inside. Hopefully they'd call the cops. "I...oh my God, I need to check on the cop. And call Carlito."

Aaron paused for a moment then nodded. "Let's go."

"I think De Fiore might be at her place. She was taking me there. It's around the corner." Tegan pointed toward the end of the street. "It's not even a block down."

Aaron pulled out a pistol before he stood and yanked the woman to her feet. Keeping her wrists secured, he marched her back to Tegan's, ignoring Gina's protests as he propelled her. He was vigilant, looking over his shoulder and scanning the street like a trained warrior.

She couldn't believe he'd showed up but she was grateful he had. Emotion clogged her throat but she shoved it back down. Now wasn't the time to lose her cool.

"My cell's in my jacket pocket," he said.

She fished it out as they hurried back to her place, and avoided looking at Gina. She immediately called

Carlito, her pulse hammering in her throat. If Enzo was truly at Gina's, the cops could arrest him now and her nightmare would finally be over.

CHAPTER NINE

Tegan sat in the cushy chair in front of Carlito's desk, watching Aaron pace back and forth like a caged wolf. After the cavalry had arrived and arrested Gina—and subsequently the SWAT team had stormed the woman's rented house and also arrested the not-so-dead Enzo De Fiore—they'd been taken to the police department. The FBI were currently foaming at the mouth trying to take De Fiore into their custody while Gina—whose real name was apparently Grace Gambino—was being interrogated by Carlito and another detective.

Tegan had answered dozens of questions from a detective and so had Aaron. They'd been separated, of course, but as of a few minutes ago, they'd basically both been dumped in Carlito's office.

Aaron had barely said two words to her. Watching him now felt like watching an angry predator. He wore a beige cable-knit sweater and dark slacks. The sweater sleeves were shoved up to his elbows, showing off all those sinewy muscles and striations. But he wouldn't look at her, as if he couldn't stand to. Instead, he simply paced. The divide between them was shredding her up inside but she wasn't sure what to say.

She'd been held at gunpoint, and had discovered the man she'd thought dead was really alive and after her again. She'd been so certain she would die. Right now she was about to crawl out of her skin at the silence. It was the first time they'd been alone since he'd tackled Gina—gah, Grace.

Finally, she couldn't handle it anymore. "I didn't mean any of those things I said!" She didn't mean to shout, but the words just came out angry and desperate as she surged to her feet. She couldn't take this silent treatment. She was barely keeping it together as it was.

He stopped pacing to turn and look at her. The little flecks of amber in his eyes seemed to be almost glowing, which she knew was ridiculous, but he was angry and it was clear in every line of his body. "You think that's why I'm pissed?"

"I...yes." She faltered because he was looking at her as if she was out of her mind.

He took a few steps toward her, but his movements weren't normal. No, he was stalking her, as if she were a little bunny and he were the big bad wolf that was going to devour her. "You left a fucking note." His voice was eerily calm.

"Well...yeah. I didn't want to just leave." And she couldn't use her stupid cell phone. Gah, she really needed to get a TracFone for emergencies. Or maybe she could even start using her own phone now. It was too soon to know yet what threat was still out there.

"A pathetic fucking note that had me going out of my mind. You should have waited until I'd gotten back and we could have come up with a game plan."

"That's exactly why I didn't wait. I knew you'd try to talk me out of leaving, and likely succeed. If anything happened to you or Dillon because of me..." Her voice cracked on the last word as the memory of that voice mail message played over in her mind. "You didn't hear that message! It was awful. He threatened Brendan and Kimmy. I..." She couldn't continue, couldn't force any more words out as her throat closed up.

"No! Don't fucking cry!" His expression was a mix of anger and horror as he took another step toward her. "Please don't cry, baby."

"I'm not crying," she muttered, wiping away the tears that started to fall down her cheeks. Damn it. What the hell? Until recently she almost never cried. Now it was like her tear ducts were permanently malfunctioning.

Suddenly his arms were around her, his quiet strength soothing her as he pulled her close. "Hell, Tegan, *please* don't cry."

She sniffled against his shirt before turning her cheek against his chest. His heartbeat was solid, steady. "I didn't know what else to do. I just knew I needed to get out of your place. I couldn't make you guys a target." She'd do it again, too, but left that part out, knowing it would just annoy him.

He stroked a gentle hand down her back, up and down, the action soothing and sweet. "I got a call from Carlito right as I got your note. Felt as if my world had imploded. I...thought you might just go on the run again." He stepped back but kept his arms around her, never letting her go. "I thought you might be gone for good," he rasped out.

She looked up at him. "I wouldn't have done that. I called Porter and he said he'd set me up with a safe house. I was going to call you as soon as I settled in."

His expression was tight. "I thought I wouldn't see you again. I panicked."

She knew he'd dropped Dillon off at his parents' place before storming over to hers. Thank God he had, too. "You saved my life. I don't know if I ever thanked you."

He made a sort of growling sound before he kissed her, hard and definitely claiming. At least that's sure how it felt. This man completely owned her when he took her mouth, kissing her until her knees felt weak and she was clutching his shoulders for support.

The sound of a throat clearing made her jerk back. She hadn't even heard the office door opening and clearly neither had Aaron. Somehow, she figured that lack of awareness was out of character for him. Good to know he was just as affected as she was.

Carlito stood there, his face neutral. At least he didn't look like the Grim Reaper. Maybe that meant something good. Like, maybe De Fiore had signed a full confession and apologized for all the pain and suffering he'd caused over the years. She nearly snorted at the ridiculous thought. Yeah, right.

"What've you got?" Aaron demanded.

"Good-ish news. Grace is ready to confess to pretty much everything in exchange for immunity."

Rage surged through Tegan. She started to speak when the detective held up his hand.

"We're not giving her full immunity. She won't do jail time but she'll be under house arrest for a long damn time. I know it's not what you were hoping for, but the Feds want De Fiore and she's serving him up on a silver platter. We're working together on this and"—he spread his hands out apologetically, and by his expression she could tell he truly was sorry—"they're calling the shots on how it plays out." That was anger in his voice.

"So she walks?" Tegan asked. "After holding a gun on me, kidnapping me, and knocking out one of your guys? Isn't that assault on a police officer or something?"

"She's not walking exactly but...yeah, it fucking blows." He rubbed a hand over his face. "But this is the way the system works sometimes. Enzo will go to jail forever. She's got a lot on him—her backup plan in case she ever got arrested. You won't be looking over your shoulder for the rest of your life. Grace doesn't give a shit about you, and all her movements will be monitored by a tracking device. She might not be going to jail but her life will be seriously altered."

Tegan leaned into Aaron, tension curling through her, tearing at her insides. He hadn't said anything about the bombing, and as far as she was concerned, De Fiore might not have been behind it.

As if he'd read her mind, Carlito continued. "Grace has been clear that Enzo never meant to hurt you in that car bombing. It was just a scare tactic."

She blinked in surprise. She hadn't been expecting De Fiore to be behind it.

"What does De Fiore say?" Aaron asked quietly. His hold around her shoulders tightened.

Carlito's lips pulled into a thin line. "Not a damn thing. Won't talk until his lawyer gets here. The guy's flying in from Chicago, so until then he's staying silent."

"We free to go?" Aaron's tone said that they'd be leaving no matter what Carlito said.

The detective nodded. "We might have more questions."

"You know where to find us. Tegan's staying with me tonight." There was no give in his words or body language.

Yeah, she wasn't going to argue with that. She released a breath she hadn't realized she'd been holding. She was tired of being afraid—*tired* being a pathetic word to describe anything. It was as if the weight that had been shoving her down for years had finally been lifted. She could breathe normally again for the first time in what felt like forever.

"You guys need an escort?" Carlito asked.

Aaron shook his head. "Red Stone's sent a security team down here to get us through the media circus. They'll be waiting at one of the back exits. You ready?" he asked her, not even waiting for Carlito to respond.

All she could do was nod. This nightmare was finally over. Now, maybe, she and Aaron might have a chance at something real. She still wasn't certain she was ready for a family, wasn't sure she had the right skills to deal with one, but she didn't want to let Aaron go.

CHAPTER TEN

"How's Dillon?" Tegan asked, after sipping the mug of tea he'd set in front of her. Aaron had bought a variety of teas since she'd been staying with him.

"Good. Sleeping." He wasn't surprised, not with the stomach bug Dillon had. He set his cell phone on the kitchen counter and drank in the sight of her. "I'm going to let him stay at my parents' tonight." It didn't seem like just this morning he'd taken Dillon to the walk-in clinic to get him checked out. So much had happened since then. They'd spent hours at the police station answering stupid questions from both the police and the FBI. He should be exhausted. Instead he was keyed up. He couldn't get a read on Tegan, though. It was frustrating.

Lord, the woman in general frustrated him even as he wanted her more than his next breath. He understood her reason for running. Hell, he respected it. She'd wanted to keep him and his son safe. But he'd thought they were starting something amazing together, and now he couldn't read her at all.

She frowned. "I hate that his schedule has been all messed up because of me."

Aaron lifted a shoulder. "It hasn't. Not really. He's on Christmas break right now and he's at my parents' every other day, it seems. If I'm on an out-of-town security detail, he stays with them. Trust me, he's fine." That was something he'd learned early on as a parent. Kids were adaptable. More so than adults.

"Oh. Good." She tapped her finger against the counter, watching him with an unreadable expression.

"What?" He rounded the island, not wanting any space between them.

She swiveled in her seat as he approached, keeping her mug in her hand. It looked an awful lot like a barrier. "Nothing. Just wondering...where we go from here."

To his bedroom or any flat surface, if she was willing. He kept that thought to himself. For now. It didn't matter that he was dying to strip her, taste and tease all of her before fully claiming her; they clearly weren't on the same page right now.

Almost losing her today drove home the conclusion he'd already come to. He wanted something real with her. And now that the threat from Enzo was over, he didn't want to keep a relationship quiet either. "I'd like to take you on a real date. Then another one and another. And if you don't have plans, I hope you'll join us for Christmas dinner in a couple weeks."

Her bright blue eyes widened. "What will we tell Dillon?"

"What do you want to tell him?" He sat in the chair next to her, even though he wanted to take the mug from her hands and pull her into his lap.

"I don't know yet. I like you...a lot. But I know you two come as a package deal."

"Do you not want..." He tried to think of the right way to ask what needed to be said. "Am I not an option for a relationship because of my son?"

She paused for so long he was sure she wouldn't answer. Dread curled in his stomach. He'd never considered that this was a real issue for her. When she'd thrown out the excuse of him being a dad, he'd thought...hell, it didn't matter.

Finally, she cleared her throat. "Not in the way you think. My mom wasn't exactly present. She dragged my brother and me around everywhere. She was rarely home and when she was, she didn't care about us. She wasn't abusive, not physically anyway. It was clear she'd have been happier if we weren't around, dragging her down."

Aaron took the mug from her hands and set it on the counter. Though he still wanted to pull her into his arms, he captured her hands in his. "I'm sorry."

"I'm just telling you so you know that I know zero about kids. I'm not the best female role model for a kid is what I'm trying to say. And I don't want to be in his life, then suddenly not be there when we break up."

He stiffened at her words. "When?"

"Okay, *if*, but you know what I mean. I'd hate to cause him any pain."

He nodded because he did. It only made him care for her more. She was concerned about Dillon's welfare in all this. How could he not adore this woman? "I've never brought any women into Dillon's life. I...haven't had any women in my life anyway. Not since..." He cleared his throat. "So I understand your concerns. I have them, too.

But what I feel for you isn't casual. I want exclusive. If we need to play the 'we're just friends' game in front of people for a while, then I'll do it. Not because I want to, but I'll do it for you."

She tightened her hands around his. "No, I don't want that. To be just friends, I mean. I really like you. After today I feel like I should hold onto you and never let go." Her cheeks flushed pink. "But maybe around Dillon we don't put a label on you and me. Other than friends. For now, anyway. I just...I never want to hurt that kid."

Aaron scrubbed a hand over his face. She said the absolute perfect thing and he knew she wasn't trying. He wasn't letting her go and as far as he was concerned, they wouldn't be breaking up. She'd woken something up inside him, made him feel alive, and he wasn't stupid enough to let her go.

"Come to bed with me tonight?" It came out more like a plea than anything but he didn't care. He needed this woman like he needed his next breath. He wasn't even sure they were at that point yet—well, *he* was at that point. But she'd been through a hell of a lot recently.

Her eyes went heavy-lidded as she got off the chair and moved to stand between his spread legs. Wordlessly she slid her hands up and around the back of his neck, linking her fingers together.

He settled his hands on her hips and tightened his grip. For a long moment he just stared at her. Her eyes were dilated and her breathing was erratic.

His own heart was beating out of control as he looked into her bright blue eyes. After months of holding back, of denying what she meant to him, he was walking a tightrope of control. Now that he had her within his grasp it was hard to think straight.

He reached down and grabbed her ass. She let out a yelp of surprise as he hoisted her up, but she didn't pause as she wrapped her legs around him.

He crushed his mouth to hers, wordlessly demanding everything from her. After tonight he knew there would be no going back for him. As her tongue teased against his, he walked them out of the kitchen, her lithe body plastered to him.

Very soon they were going to be skin to skin. His body shuddered as he thought of it, of finally having her completely bared to him.

When they reached the foyer, he paused by the bottom of the stairs then veered into the living room. They weren't going to make it to the bedroom.

The Christmas tree lights and the faux fire from the fireplace gave them more than enough illumination. It would let him see her fully, as he needed right now. As they passed the couch, he blindly reached out and grabbed some of the blankets.

Somehow he tore his mouth from hers. "In here okay?" It seemed those were the only words he could force out.

"Oh yeah." The heat in her voice slid through and around him.

He worked quickly to toss the blankets on the floor before tugging her down onto them.

Laughing, she tumbled onto the blankets and cupped his face. "I'm not going anywhere, Aaron," she whispered.

He just nodded. Hearing the words did a little to soothe all his jagged edges, but not much. Almost frantic, he tugged her jeans off to reveal tiny black panties barely covering her mound. The twinkly lights from the tree played off her smooth ivory skin, and her auburn hair seemed brighter.

Part of him wanted to carry her upstairs to his bed but he needed to be in her right this second. Before he could make a move to finish undressing her, she pushed up and stripped off her sweater. Her tiny black bra barely covered breasts he'd been fantasizing about for way too long.

He could see the outline of her hard nipples through the lacy material. When his gaze finally strayed back up to her face, he found her watching him with a sensual half smile.

"You have this look on your face, like you want to..." Even in the dimly lit living room he could see her cheeks flush that sexy shade of pink.

His cock pressed insistently against his pants. Too fucking bad for him. "What?" he murmured. "Like I want to eat you?"

She made a sort of coughing sound as she nodded. There was an innocent quality about her that he adored. Last night when he'd told her what he'd wanted to do to her, how he'd wanted to shove her dress up and eat her pussy, he'd loved getting a reaction out of her, loved seeing that sweet blush on her cheeks. Tonight he wasn't going to stop at just tasting her. He was going to fully claim her, show her how good they could be together.

Tegan watched as Aaron lifted one of her legs and brought her ankle to his mouth. He kept his gaze on hers the entire time as he raked his teeth over a section of skin she'd never thought was sensitive.

But the oh-so-gentle way his teeth grazed her skin sent shivers skating through her. She felt vulnerable, stretched out in just her underwear while he was still fully dressed. She wanted to reach for him, to strip his clothes off so that nothing was between them, but it was clear he was taking charge right now.

And, yeah, it was pretty hot.

Everything about Aaron melted her, right down to the way he listened to her concerns about broadcasting their relationship to his son. She'd met a lot of people during her time on the run and he was truly one of the best men she'd ever known. It was too soon to say the L word, but she knew she was heading that way fast, if she wasn't there already. Because the deepest part of her trusted him, was connected to him in a way she couldn't put into words.

He reached her knee, kissing her slowly, following up with his teeth. He had his other hand on her opposite leg, holding her thighs open for him.

On instinct she spread them wider. Heat flooded her core with each kiss, each nip of his talented, wicked mouth. As she remembered what he'd done to her last night, another rush of need filled her. The man made her feel things she'd hadn't in...ever. He made her feel alive and grounded at the same time.

Everything about him was solid—hers.

She moaned when he crawled higher, reaching her inner thigh. Her legs were trembling as he took his sweet time teasing her.

She slid her fingers through his hair and held onto his head tight, dying for the moment he put his mouth to her folds.

"Tell me what you want, baby," he murmured, his teeth nipping at one of her most sensitive spots. The soft skin of her inner thigh seemed to have a thousand nerve endings as he focused on it—probably because all she wanted him to do was shove her panties to the side and give her what she needed.

He was clearly enjoying teasing her.

"To come," she rasped out. With him. She desperately wanted to feel him inside her, for him to find release, too. She loved what they'd shared last night but she needed more and she knew he did as well.

He chuckled against her skin; the sound a little bit wicked. Instead of responding, he teased her soaked panties to the side and barely skimmed his finger along her folds—and nowhere near her clit. "Do better than that." His words were a bare whisper.

She rolled her hips, needing so much more. "Your mouth on my clit."

He growled softly, the sound reverberating through her. His tongue flicked out, barely grazing her clit.

"Aaron." His name tore from her lips.

That was apparently all the motivation he needed because he sucked on her clit, making her jerk against his face. She shouldn't be this close yet, but she was already on edge just being around him, thinking about what might have happened, and she wanted everything from him. When he fully slid his finger inside her, she grabbed onto his shoulders. Yes, this was what she needed.

The man had learned her body so quickly and she couldn't wait for him to fill her.

He added another finger and began thrusting inside her, his movements so gentle, so smooth. It was too much and not enough. She didn't want his fingers. She wanted his cock.

She squeezed his shoulders tight, dragging at his sweater. She needed him naked right freaking now. "Aaron."

He paused and looked up at her with the gleam of a predator in his gaze. She shivered at the intensity, more than happy to be his prey.

Her hands stilled at the hem of his sweater. "I want to come with you inside me."

It was like her words set him off. His big body shuddered. Still crouched between her legs, he stripped his sweater off and tossed it behind him.

Her breath caught in her throat as she devoured the sight of him finally bared to her. For months she'd wondered what he had under the dark suit he normally wore to the shop. She wanted to grip his broad shoulders or muscular arms as she rode him. Or hold on tight as he pinned her to the soft blanket by the Christmas tree.

She was surprised to see a tattoo on his left pec, one of an eagle, globe, and anchor, the Marine Corps symbol. The tattoo only made him hotter, something she hadn't thought possible. He was already off the charts making her crazy.

She continued staring as he shifted slightly and finished stripping, losing his pants and boxers in a few fluid moves.

She'd been lucky enough to hold his cock last night, to stroke him to orgasm, but he'd still been mostly dressed and he'd finished himself off. Seeing him on his knees, that thick length jutting forward, and the tree lights highlighting all his perfection was enough to render her speechless.

He didn't seem to mind as he crawled on the blanket toward her, moving with a sleekness that told her exactly how strong and capable he was.

She shuddered as he covered her body with his, caging her in with his arms. His breathing was harsh as he stared down at her. Lust shone in his dark eyes so clearly it stole her breath.

Hungrily, she reached for him, stroking over his chest and arms, desperate to explore every inch of his muscular, toned body.

"This thing I feel for you...I've never felt like this about anyone, Tegan." The words came out guttural.

The truth of his words rocketed through her. She felt the same way but couldn't find her voice, could barely think straight. She didn't trust her voice anyway. Though the truth was part of her was afraid this would all be ripped away from her. That he was too good to be true. She'd been on the run, alone for so long, she was terrified that she wanted him too much. And because she did, she'd lose him. As if the universe were just waiting to kick her one more time. To give her everything she wanted, then take it away.

For now, she shoved that fear aside and focused on the here and now. On him. Reaching between their bodies, she wrapped her fingers around his hard length. He pulsed in her grip, his hips rolling into her hold.

She stroked him slowly, holding tight like she'd discovered he liked last night. That one time with him wasn't enough—it barely counted in her book. She needed all of him so badly she was trembling with the need. It had been over two years for her, something she'd confessed to him last night when they'd been lying on his couches, with Dillon fast asleep. It had just been the two of them awake, talking.

He'd admitted it had been way longer for him. As in, since his ex. So while she was desperate for him, she was also a little nervous. It felt like a big deal to be his first since—

He crushed his mouth to hers, splintering those stupid worries and scattering them to the wind as he took over.

As he flicked his tongue against hers, he reached between their bodies and grasped her wrist, tugging her hand from his cock.

She started to protest until he guided both her hands above her head, stretching her out fully underneath him. She loved the feel of being pinned beneath him as he held her wrists in place.

Arching into him, she moaned into his mouth and wrapped her legs around him. The feel of her breasts against his chest, his cock against her stomach, the skin-to-skin contact, made her feel alive.

"I want to touch you everywhere," he murmured against her lips, his mouth still skating against hers.

She rolled her hips against him in response. How was he even talking, thinking? Her inner walls ached, needing to be filled by him.

He nibbled a slow path along her jaw, reaching between their bodies with his free hand and cupping one of her breasts. "I thought about this so many damn times," he rasped out. "Every time I saw you in the shop, every time you made a smartass comment. All I could think about was this."

"Yeah?" She wanted to know what his fantasies were, but couldn't force the question out.

"I thought about bending you over one of the display cases, pushing into you from behind." He tweaked a nipple, rolling it between his fingers in a sensual move.

Combined with his words, heat flooded between her thighs. "Do it now. Bend me over."

He stilled, lifting his head slightly to look at her. She squeezed her legs once around his waist then let go, letting them fall to the soft blanket.

He shoved up on his arms, still caging her in with that huge, sexy body. He looked a little uncertain, as if he wasn't sure this was what she wanted. How could he ever doubt?

Wordlessly, she rolled over and moved onto her stomach. Before she could push up, he wrapped an arm around her middle and tugged her to her knees and back against him. His cock was hard against her behind.

She clenched her fingers into the blanket as he smoothed a hand over her ass.

"You are fucking perfection," he murmured. He tested her slickness with a finger before pushing inside her so slowly, making her crazy.

His thick length pushed deeper, deeper, until a moan tore free from her throat. "God, Aaron." There were no words left.

She felt consumed by him. For so many years she'd been on the run, moving from place to place, looking over her shoulder and waiting to get a bullet in the head. Now it was as if she'd been running straight for Aaron and hadn't even known it. She was still scared that things wouldn't work out, but she couldn't be a coward any longer and not take a chance on him.

On them.

She knew this kind of connection was rare, that what they could have was special. And she'd be the worst kind of coward if she ran from him.

She arched back as he reached around, cupping one of her breasts, tweaking and teasing her nipple as he thrust over and over. Pleasure poured through her as he took her, battering at her nerve endings.

He was just a little rough, a little on edge, and she loved it. He'd always seemed so rigid, so in control until recently and this was the best surprise of all. That and his dirty talk from last night.

She grew slicker the harder he pushed, turned on by the groaning sounds he made. His other hand tightened once around her hip, his hold hard enough that he'd probably leave a bruise. Some primal part of her she hadn't even known existed was excited at the thought.

When his hand slid around her and cupped her mound, strumming her clit, her entire body jolted in awareness.

"Faster," she moaned. She just needed him to speed up and—she surged into orgasm, her inner walls tightening around him like a vise as the pleasure speared out to all her nerve endings.

He must have been holding back because as soon as she let go, he did the same, her name a rough growl on his lips.

She clutched at the blanket, her fingers tightening into the material as over and over he continued thrusting inside her. Her entire body felt oversensitive, like one big nerve ending as her climax seemed to go on forever.

They both collapsed onto the blanket almost in unison. Thankfully he rolled off her and sidled up next to her. Lying flat on her stomach, she turned her head to look at him since that was all the energy she had at the moment.

He was on his side, his head propped in one hand. Leaning over, he brushed his mouth against her forehead, the action sweetly sensual. She could feel the possessiveness humming through him when he kissed her.

He smoothed a hand down her back, lightly stroking against her spine. She shivered at the contact and he immediately grabbed another blanket draped across the nearby ottoman and pulled it over them.

She finally moved, curling against his chest as he stretched out onto his back. The lights twinkled beside them, casting shadows around the room. For the first time in years she felt safe, whole. All because of the man next to her.

She wasn't sure how long they lay there, and didn't really care. "When I was on the run, it was hard." The words were out before she could think about what she was saying, or how much she was opening up.

His grip tightened ever so slightly around her, but he didn't respond. He was simply silent so she could get the words out.

Tegan was grateful he was letting her open up. "I...sometimes had to do things I wasn't proud of. I pretty much left with the clothes on my back and a few suitcases. A couple times a year I...stole license plates to switch them out with mine so it would be harder to track me." She still felt guilty about that.

"That's smart."

She huffed out a laugh at his words, surprised there was no recrimination there. "In the first six months it was really hard even though I'd done the backpacking thing before. A couple motels I skipped out on paying because I was scared what little money I had wouldn't be enough to cover me until the next town."

His grip tightened again, his lips brushing over the top of her head. "You're incredible, Tegan." Sincerity laced his words.

She'd expected...well, she wasn't sure what she'd expected—him to judge her, maybe. Looking up at him, she met his gaze. "I think we should just lie here all night," she murmured.

"That sounds like a good idea to me." His voice was just as quiet as he watched her, that familiar intense look in place.

She was glad he felt that way because there was nowhere else she wanted to be.

CHAPTER ELEVEN

A thrill shot through Alec to see Tegan O'Kelly leaving the police station on the news. A man was with the redhead and there appeared to be a group of security escorting them...cops off duty, maybe?

It was hard to tell. But he recognized the face of the man from his files. Aaron Fitzpatrick went into Kimmy's Cakes and Coffee occasionally.

From the phone records Alec had acquired, it didn't appear that Tegan had ever had contact with the man so he hadn't even been on the radar as someone important. But the images on screen didn't lie, and that man was very much invested in Tegan's safety. Every movement he made was designed to protect her from harm. It was the way the man carried himself, the way he blocked her from everything. And the expression on his face when he glanced at her...they were definitely in a relationship.

There had been a couple of calls from Fitzpatrick's house directly to the coffee shop recently. Alec had been monitoring the shop's phone but hadn't thought anything of it since that phone number belonged to the brother of the man the shop owner was likely fucking.

This was all very interesting.

Now that Enzo and that bitch Grace had been arrested, Alec knew he'd have to act fast. Because something told him Grace wouldn't keep her mouth shut. No matter how hardcore she liked to act, she'd sell Enzo out—and Enzo might be tempted to sell out someone else higher up the food chain in an effort to reduce his sentence. Which meant Alec's boss would be under the microscope and, subsequently, Alec would be, too. That was unacceptable.

So he still had to kill Tegan. Now that the Feds knew Enzo was alive, this was even better. Alec would kill Tegan and lead an obvious money trail back to Enzo, 'proving' that Enzo had hired someone to kill the woman. It wouldn't matter if Enzo tried to cut a deal with the Feds once that became public knowledge.

If the FBI made a deal with him after a woman like Tegan O'Kelly got murdered on Enzo's orders, a sweet woman who worked in a coffee shop and had already survived a bombing, the public would go crazy for blood. The FBI only liked to be in the news if they were being praised.

Yes, yes, this could work. Alec would even get a bonus for this. He'd been sent to kill the woman so Enzo would never know that she *wasn't* the one who took those diamonds. Now her death would work even more in his favor. It would ensure Enzo went away forever, maybe even got the death penalty.

Pulling up his laptop, he worked fast, typing in commands. Her phone still wasn't turned on, but he'd find her. Now that he had a pretty good idea of who she'd been staying with, or at least had a relationship with, hunting her down would be easy enough.

Then he'd kill her, make it look as if Enzo had ordered it, and leave a trail as wide as the Grand fucking

Canyon back to the old fool. It wouldn't even need to be spectacular. Just a clean kill. Sure, the Feds would attempt to hunt Alec down after he killed her, but he wouldn't leave an evidence trail to himself. He never did. He'd just ghost out of town.

So Enzo would go away for the murder and the Feds would just have to be happy with Enzo. Because they'd never catch him. Alec was too good for them, always had been. And taking on one woman would be one of the easiest kills he'd ever done once he caught up to her. She had no training.

After she was finally dead, Alec's boss would be happy. Everyone would win. Everyone except a pretty redhead who should have died years ago.

* * *

"Higher!" Dillon squealed as Tegan pushed him on the swing, his excitement infectious.

Aaron, standing with her, leaned over and kissed her cheek. "Gonna hit the head. I'll be back in a few."

She smiled at him, feeling light and free for the first time in years. "We're not going anywhere."

Kali danced around the big swing set, thrilled to be out and playing. The park was mostly empty and for the first time in years she knew she was safe. Well, as safe as anyone could be. No one was hunting her. She was outside, breathing fresh air and free from the worries of the last couple of years. Dillon and Aaron were safe. All her friends were okay. Enzo De Fiore was in custody and not going anywhere.

As Aaron headed down the winding walkway, he turned and half waved before he disappeared behind one of the jungle gyms on his way to the washroom. The park was massive and she was surprised there weren't more people there, especially since it was a Sunday. Maybe people were sleeping in since there had been a cold snap overnight.

Of course, Florida cold compared to some of the places she'd lived wasn't too terrible. To her it was invigorating. There was no snow on the ground but there was an icy nip in the air that made her think of sitting in front of a crackling fire and sipping hot cocoa—with a certain sexy man at her side.

"You want to walk to Kimmy's shop and get some cocoa after this?" Tegan asked Dillon amidst his shouts of "higher, higher." The park they were at was only a few blocks away from the strip of shops where Kimmy's place was located. Tegan wanted to stop by the Mederos family's restaurant and Julieta's shop, too, to see everyone who'd been so concerned about her and thank them for all the food they'd sent.

"Yes!" he shouted. He seemed to be in 'shout mode,' as Aaron had called it earlier this morning when Bree had dropped him off.

Apparently whatever virus he'd had was long gone and the kid was full of energy. Aaron had told her it was normal, that was just how kids were. They bounced back like nothing had ever happened.

Even though all her worries about Enzo were gone, there was still a little niggle at the back of her mind that something was going to go wrong. That this bit of happiness she'd found would disappear. Logically, she knew it was a learned response because she'd lived in fear for so long. She wasn't actually anticipating danger.

"I want to go on the merry-go-round!"

"Okay." Laughing, Tegan stopped pushing and let the swing start to slow.

She glanced around the park again, unable to shake that weird feeling in the pit of her stomach. A mother was on a bench while her two kids raced across monkey bars. Another mom stood next to a small toddler attempting to climb onto the head of a big plastic fish that had been made to look as if it was coming out of the ground. It was in the middle of a big circular section with soft, squishy material instead of concrete where different plastic sea life sprouted from it. When Tegan had asked Dillon if he wanted to play there, he'd looked at her so seriously and told her he was a big boy now and that section was for babies.

Rolling her shoulders once in an attempt to get rid of the residual tension, she reached for the seat of the swing and stilled it completely so Dillon could slide out.

"Daddy said you're coming to Christmas dinner with us this year," Dillon said, tucking his little hand into hers.

The trusting action seemed so natural for him and it warmed her better than any hot chocolate ever could. She still felt like she was navigating foreign terrain where kids were concerned but so far Dillon seemed to like her. "Yes, he asked me to. Is that okay with you?"

Kali fell into place next to them, prancing as only she could as they made their way to the merry-go-round.

He grinned up at her. "Yep. I even got you a present."

She blinked. "You did?" Oh, crap. She needed to get them presents. With everything going on she hadn't even thought about Christmas. Not really. The holiday had been in her face since November with decorations all over the city and on television but it had been an abstract thing for her. She hadn't thought about Christmas because she'd planned to be alone again this year. For her, holidays had never been a particularly fun time of year. Her mom had barely put in a half-ass attempt to celebrate with her and her brother. Forget about lights or a tree. She and her brother had always gotten one present for each other but that had been the extent of their holiday celebration. After her mother had died, Tegan hadn't really cared to put in much effort either. She'd usually just done something with her single friends.

"Yep. It's awesome, too." He continued chattering, telling her about what he'd gotten his daddy for Christmas and how he hoped Santa brought him Thor's hammer. It took her a moment to realize it was a reference to *The Avengers*.

As they headed across a grassy incline, an SUV slowly steered through the parking lot. The windows were tinted dark. On the back she saw one of those little stick family sticker collections, including a dog.

She glanced over her shoulder, looking for Aaron. The place was big but he'd find them. Still, she wished he was with them.

God, she had to get over whatever this weird anxiousness was. After the bombing, the doctor had mentioned she might have some lingering effects, including panic attacks. Maybe she really did need to talk to someone. The thought of opening up to a complete stranger felt weird, though.

As they reached the merry-go-round, she glanced over as the SUV backed into a parking spot. The parking lot spanned around three sides of the park and everyone had parked by the main entrance, their vehicles clustered together. This driver parked about twenty spaces away from the other vehicles.

"Spin me!"

Tegan started spinning Dillon as a man wearing a sweatshirt, jogging pants, and a black knitted cap got out of the SUV. When he started stretching she realized he was going to use the running track that looped through the park. Rolling her eyes at herself, she turned back to the merry-go-round where Dillon was still hanging on and giggling.

A smile broke over her face—until she saw a man jogging across the other side of the parking lot in their direction. He was coming from a nondescript truck parked far away from everyone else. It took all of a second for her to recognize the man. She didn't know his name but she knew that face. A large scar slashed over his left cheek on a ragged angle, almost looking like a sideways V covering most of his cheek. It was very memorable.

Terror jolted through her, the jagged lightning bolt edges making her freeze for a moment.

A sidewalk and fence separated them but he was moving in their direction with purpose.

Everything funneled out as she jerked the merry-go-round to a halt. "Dillon, come here. We've gotta go now."

Next to her Kali whined, maybe because she sensed Tegan's tension. There was still no sign of Aaron.

"We'll get ice cream and whatever you want. Come on—" She stopped talking as the man's gaze connected with hers.

She yanked Dillon into her arms, ready to run. The man broke into a sprint. Without pause, she started running, Dillon wrapped around her like a little monkey.

Her heart was in her throat as she tore over the grass. "That man's bad. We've gotta find your daddy. If I tell you to run and hide, you've got to listen. Okay?" Her words were coming out in gasps, her heart galloping in her chest as she raced toward the two buildings in the middle of the park. That was where Aaron had gone.

"Okay," Dillon whispered, fear flickering across his features.

"Aaron!" she screamed, not caring that she looked like a crazy person. She didn't care about anything other than getting Dillon to safety. "Aaron!" His name tore from her throat. She knew she sounded like a savage animal.

Dillon stared at her wide-eyed but just clutched her tighter. Kali growled low in her throat as she ran next to them. Oh God, where was Aaron?

One of the moms screamed. "He's got a gun!"

Panic exploded inside her as they raced past one of the jungle gyms. She glanced over her shoulder to see the man jumping the fence, a huge pistol in his hand.

Adrenaline rocketed through her as a shot rang out. She braced for pain, for an impact, but felt nothing.

She didn't slow down as she sprinted, but the restrooms were too far. Holding Dillon tight she raced toward a cluster of trees. Clumps of dirt flew up in the air as she veered to the left.

Screaming Aaron's name again, she dove behind a huge oak as wood splintered inches from her head.

* * *

Aaron leaned against the brick wall exterior of the multi-bathroom building, his cell phone to his ear as he talked to Porter. "Yeah, I'll be good to go in a week. I still want to take off the next few days—"

"Aaron!" The sound of Tegan's scream made all the hair on the back of his neck stand up. Aaron shoved away from the wall, pocketing his phone as he withdrew his weapon in a fluid, practiced move. Fear gripped his chest. His son and Tegan were out there. Years of training kicked in.

"He's got a gun!" A woman's terrified scream ripped through the air.

Adrenaline poured through him as he raced toward the woman's and Tegan's cries. He had to get to Dillon and Tegan.

When he heard the sound of gunfire, only years of training forced him to slow down as he reached the end of the brick wall. Weapon out and crouching low, he peered around the corner of the building.

For a moment he froze, all the muscles in his body tightening. Tegan and Dillon were huddled behind a tree as a man with a SIG raced toward them.

There was no cover for Aaron, but he was going to take this guy down before he got to Tegan and Dillon. There was no other option.

He'd keep his son and the woman he loved safe.

Suddenly Kali burst out from behind the jungle gym, a rabid, feral warrior that looked nothing like the sweet husky she was. She was racing for the gunman at full speed. The man turned to the left, facing the threat and putting his back to Aaron.

On a burst of speed, Aaron raced for them as Kali lunged at the gunman. Shots rang out as Kali jumped into the air. Everything else around Aaron funneled out as Kali slammed the man to the ground. The SIG went flying so Aaron kicked it out of the way as he reached them.

The man was unmoving under a motionless Kali. *Oh God.*

There was no time to check on the dog. He needed to secure the threat immediately. Keep Tegan and Dillon safe.

Before he could move, the man kicked out with a snarl, knocking Aaron's feet from under him. Aaron fell back as the man jerked up, shoving the dog off him.

Blood soaked the man's hoodie. He lunged at Aaron.

Aaron went on the offensive, slamming his fist against the guy's jaw. It didn't slow the asshole down. With fevered, dark eyes he swung at Aaron.

Aaron ducked his head to the side and rolled to his feet. He didn't want to kill the guy, but he would if he had to. He aimed his weapon at him. "Don't fucking move," he snarled.

The man was on one knee, calculation in his gaze. He had to have another weapon.

Aaron's aim was steady. He would absolutely shoot this son of a bitch if he had to. "Go for it. See who gets off a shot first."

Something like resignation flared in the man's eyes. He lifted his hands in the air and lay flat on his belly. "I've got a gun in my ankle holster and a knife at my back." Breathing heavily, he turned his face to the side against the grass.

Gone was the fighter from moments before but Aaron wasn't going to let himself be lulled into a false sense of security. He didn't bother disarming the guy. He had faith in his abilities to disarm him, but he wasn't risking it right now. With Dillon and Tegan so close, he wasn't going to take the chance that the guy would attack when he got Aaron at closer range. Anything could happen in a split second. He'd wait for the cops to get here and do their job.

With his free hand he started to pull his cell phone out of his pocket when Dillon's scared voice came from behind the tree.

"Dad?"

Another surge of panic pummeled him, but he didn't take his focus off the man on the ground. "Stay where you are! Everything's fine. Just stay put."

"We're okay and we're not moving," Tegan called out, her voice shaky. "Cops are on their way. Should be here in a couple minutes."

Almost as if on cue, sirens wailed in the distance, the sound of them music to his ears. He just hoped this nightmare was finally over—and that Kali would make it. She hadn't moved since she'd been shot, but he could hear her labored breathing and she was softly whining. He hated that he couldn't help her. But he couldn't take his focus off the gunman, not for a second.

CHAPTER TWELVE

"She's going to be okay." Aaron wrapped an arm around Tegan's shoulders as they sat in the waiting room of the vet's office.

Kali was in surgery and Tegan didn't know what she'd do if her sweet dog didn't make it. Kali had been her constant companion through the crappiest moments of her life. She was young and sweet and had fought like hell to protect her and Dillon. To lose her after everything they'd gone through, after the rough start she'd had to her life...

Tegan's throat tightened and she swallowed hard because she didn't trust herself to respond. Not without having a meltdown anyway.

The front door opened and Tegan jumped. Her nerves were frayed and she couldn't take any more surprises.

Aaron straightened and stood when Carlito stepped inside.

Tegan was surprised to see him there. Her heart rate stuttered at his grim expression. She shot to her feet, tensing for the worst. "What's wrong now?"

He blinked. "Nothing. I just...how's your dog?"

"No news." She slumped back in the chair, but Aaron remained standing.

"Why are you here?" he asked quietly.

"Good-ish news. Grace lost her deal with the Feds because she lied to them about who was behind the bombing of your car."

Tegan raised her eyebrows. Now she knew that the man who'd come after them in the park was behind the bombing, not Enzo. She'd recognized him from Chicago, had seen him once talking to Enzo. While she hadn't known Alec Rossi's name, she'd known he wasn't at that park by chance, and had been there for her. "Really, she lost the deal?"

"Yeah. She'll be doing jail time. Not as much as I'm sure you'd like, but it's something. Enzo will be going away for a very long time, too."

"Why do I feel like there's a *but* in there?"

Carlito flicked a glance at Aaron once before sitting a few chairs down from them. "There is. Sorta. Alec Rossi is in federal custody. He's going to do jail time, but..."

Next to her Aaron tensed and she didn't blame him one bit. That bastard had come after her at a children's park. And he'd shot at her while she'd been running with Dillon, *a five-year-old boy.* All the muscles in Tegan's body went tight. If Carlito said he was getting some cushy deal, she was going to let any reporter who wanted to interview her do one. And she'd tell everyone exactly how screwed up their justice system was, until it was splashed all over every headline she could make.

Carlito held up a hand as he turned back to her, probably seeing the rage on her face. "He's definitely going to jail. He was hired by a man named Stefano De Fiore, Enzo's cousin."

Tegan nodded. "Yeah, I know the name. He was Enzo's second in command. I met him once." *Met* was a bit of a stretch. He'd been in the same room as her once, and when Enzo had wanted to hurt her, the cousin had made it sound like a bad idea—and convinced Enzo that it was his idea to back off. "He seemed...smarter than Enzo."

"According to Rossi, Stefano hired him to kill you when he got word Enzo was hunting you for those diamonds."

It took her a moment to digest why. "Because Stefano took them, didn't he?" Which meant Stefano had killed her brother. Or at the very least, ordered his death. Otherwise why bother coming after her? He'd needed to cover up the fact that he'd taken them in case Enzo figured out Tegan hadn't been behind the theft.

Carlito nodded, a touch of pity flickering in his gray gaze. "Yeah. And—"

"My brother is dead. Is that what you're going to tell me?" She held the tears at bay. Barely. She'd known he was gone, had known it in her heart.

Aaron silently wrapped his arm around her shoulders and held her close.

"Yeah. Rossi killed him on Stefano's orders. He was supposed to completely incinerate the body but he didn't. He kept your brother and a few others as leverage should he ever need it." He cleared his throat, his expression softening. "They're in an industrial freezer, well preserved. He knew this day might come. He's turning evidence against Stefano and giving the location of all the bodies. Those families deserve closure and so do you. And it will bring down that entire criminal empire in Chicago. I'm so sorry, Tegan. Truly."

She clenched her jaw and squeezed her hands together to stop them from shaking. Aaron just pulled her closer, his presence the only thing keeping her from breaking down. "What's he getting in return?"

"They're taking the death penalty off the table. And he gets to choose the prison he wants to go to. It'll be a supermax, high-security prison but he still gets to choose where. He'll be in solitary confinement, though. For his protection."

She and Dillon—and other innocent people at that park—could have been killed by that man. It was a miracle no one had been injured except Kali. Wetness covered her cheeks and she realized she was crying. Deep down she'd known her brother was dead but there had been that stupid, tiny spark of hope that refused to give up.

Aaron's arms were fully around her before she could blink. She buried her face in his chest, unsure how long she remained there, letting the tears come. Eventually she raised her head when she trusted herself to be able to talk again. "Why did Gina—uh, Grace, lie?"

Carlito scrubbed a hand over his handsome face. "I could give you a diplomatic answer but the truth is she's fucking stupid. From what I gather, she thought with you dead, you wouldn't be around to testify, so things would go easier on her sentencing and on Enzo. Even though she turned evidence against him, she apparently still cared enough about Enzo to try to give him that. I don't know what was going on in her head. Her lawyer's pissed at her. She has no leverage now. The woman is a fucking moron."

Tegan nodded, glad the woman would be going to jail.

She looked up at Aaron, her miracle. She didn't care if it was too soon or if she was assessing her feelings while on emotional steroids, but she loved him. Clearing her throat, she looked back at Carlito. "Glad she won't be able to get out of it. I think I know the answer, but how did Rossi find me?" She hadn't even thought to ask Carlito when the cavalry had arrived, because she'd been too worried about Kali.

He'd had an ambulance race Kali to the vet and, breaking all sorts of protocols, had let Tegan stay with Kali for the first part of her surgery. Once she'd come through the worst of it, Tegan and Aaron had gone back to the police station for a crapload of questioning and paperwork—though Carlito had gotten them out of there as fast as he could. For that she was grateful. If she never saw the inside of a police station again, it would be too soon. She was tired of people trying to kill her and tired of stupid questions.

The detective lifted a shoulder. "Your phone. He'd actually figured out who you were staying with after that clip of you on the news, leaving the station with Aaron. But he just tracked your phone to the park this morning when you turned it on. Illegal as fuck and he'll be charged with that, too. He's being charged with everything we've got. He'll never see the outside of a prison once he goes in. Hell, he's been denied bail completely so he won't have any freedom from this point forward."

Tegan nodded, her throat tight. "Thank you for coming to tell us."

"I'm just sorry for all the hell you've been through." He stood and took a step toward the door before stopping. "Now I get to go deliver the good news to Enzo in person. He'd been planning on turning evidence against his cousin. With all Rossi's information, the Feds don't need Enzo at all. He's not getting a deal. Can't wait to see the look on that fucker's face when I tell him he's going down."

Tegan blinked. "You told us before him?"

Carlito nodded, standing. "Figured you should know in person. That guy will never hurt you or anyone again. And he'll know for a fact that his own cousin betrayed him and took those diamonds. You're not on his radar anymore. You're nothing to him. He's going to spend the rest of his life behind bars, probably plotting how to kill his cousin and Rossi. I'll keep you up to date with everything."

Once Carlito was gone and the door had shut quietly behind him, Tegan's shoulders slumped and she turned toward Aaron once again. She wrapped her arms around him tight. "Thank you for everything you've done." He'd taken her into his home, kept her safe, and saved her life twice in a matter of a few short days. Her chest felt hollowed out. She couldn't take another blow—wasn't sure she could handle it. Aaron was the one bright spot in all this mess.

His grip tightened. "Don't ever thank me for that. I...I'm in love with you, Tegan. I know it's too soon and—"

Her head snapped back and she looked up at him. Emotions flickered in his dark eyes, too many to figure out. "I love you, too. So much it hurts. I love the way you are with your son. You're such a good dad and that's crazy sexy. Something I never imagined thinking. You're kind to everyone and you went out of your way to keep a virtual stranger—me—safe. Ever since then you've been a rock, someone I know I can count on no matter what. I...I just love you."

His mouth curved up in a sweet half smile but it fell as the door to the back opened. The operating room and the other rooms were back there. The vet, not her assistant, was standing there.

For one brief moment Tegan feared the worst until the vet gave her a relieved, bright smile.

"Kali's through the worst and she's going to make it."

EPILOGUE

Six months later

Tegan used her key to Aaron's place to let herself in. He'd given her a key almost immediately after Christmas but she rarely used it. Because she was seldom here when he wasn't.

He'd asked her to stop by his place and pick something up for him before meeting him at his parents' for their weekly Sunday dinner. They'd spent most of the morning together, but she'd gone home for a couple of hours because she'd needed to finish up some design stuff for her growing business. Soon she was going to have to make a decision about staying on at the coffee shop or going full time with her business. And she knew she needed to make some other decisions as well. Aaron wanted her to move in with him and Dillon but she couldn't do it. She was an old-fashioned kind of girl. She couldn't live with him until she had a ring on her finger. It was the way she was wired.

Some people didn't need that piece of paper, but she needed it. Needed the commitment it symbolized. But she hadn't told him that, hadn't wanted to put any pressure on him. She'd just told him she wasn't ready for that yet, that she was happy the way things were. Which was mostly true.

When she stepped inside Aaron's place she frowned as she shut the door behind her. The alarm hadn't gone off and she knew he was vigilant about setting it. Any fear she might have had disappeared when she turned around and saw a piece of paper on the ground with an arrow, clearly drawn and colored in by Dillon. Curiosity replaced concern.

Smiling to herself, she followed the arrow into the kitchen to find a little sign with a painted red heart and a bunch of glitter covering it on a small stand. Underneath it was another arrow pointing toward the back door. The blinds were closed on the door so she couldn't see what was out there. *What are those two up to?*

Heart pounding with excitement, she dropped her purse and keys on the counter and hurried out the back door. Aaron and Dillon stood there, smiles on their faces, and Kali beside them, tongue lolling. The back porch was decorated with a string of red heart lights and more handmade items, all Dillon's art, with drawings of the three of them holding hands—and Kali was in all of them, too.

Kali, who was back to her healthy self, trotted up to Tegan when Aaron patted her head once. A little sign hung from around her neck, attached to a red ribbon. She bent down and rubbed Kali's head as she read the sign: Pull Me. She tugged on the ribbon and a little box fell onto the ground.

She plucked it up and realized it was a jewelry box. Her heart started pounding even wilder in her chest. When she looked up, Aaron was already on one knee in front of her.

The smile was gone as he watched her with that intensity she felt all the way to her core. "I love you more than I ever thought possible. You're the best thing to happen to us. Marry me?"

Throat tight with emotion, she nodded. She tried to get the word *yes* out but tears were pouring down her face.

"I thought you'd be happy!" Dillon's stricken voice and little face made her find her voice.

"I'm so happy." She tugged him and Aaron into a big hug. "This is the best proposal ever. I love you guys!"

"You haven't even seen the ring," Dillon's voice was muffled because she was probably squeezing him too tight.

Laughing, she pulled back and brushed a kiss over Aaron's mouth. "Yes, yes, yes."

He slid the ring on her finger before she'd even had a chance to look at it. When she did glance down, her breath caught. Instead of a traditional diamond it was a cluster of their birthstones. The symbolism that they were truly a family made her chest tighten. "It's beautiful." The word seemed inadequate to describe what she truly thought of the ring. Of what it meant to her. For the first time in her life she felt like she truly was part of a family.

"You're beautiful," he murmured, the heat in his eyes a promise of what was to come later.

"Santa was pretty late, but you're the best Christmas present ever!" Dillon tackled her again in a hug.

She wrapped her arms around him, her tears slowing, and joy suffusing her entire body. Aaron joined him, wrapping his arms around both of them. "She's the most precious gift in the world."

Thank you for reading Dangerous Protector. If you don't want to miss any future releases, please feel free to join my newsletter. I only send out a newsletter for new releases or sales news. Find the signup link on my website: http://www.katiereus.com

ACKNOWLEDGMENTS

Thank you to everyone instrumental in getting this book in shape; Kari (always!), Joan, Andrea, Sarah and Jaycee. Whether it be for the edits, the behind-the-scenes stuff, or the gorgeous cover, I'm appreciative of all of it! I'm also thankful to my family for all their support. To my readers, thank you for reading my books! As always, I'm grateful to God for everything.

COMPLETE BOOKLIST

Red Stone Security Series
No One to Trust
Danger Next Door
Fatal Deception
Miami, Mistletoe & Murder
His to Protect
Breaking Her Rules
Protecting His Witness
Sinful Seduction
Under His Protection
Deadly Fallout
Sworn to Protect
Secret Obsession
Love Thy Enemy
Dangerous Protector

The Serafina: Sin City Series
First Surrender
Sensual Surrender
Sweetest Surrender
Dangerous Surrender

Deadly Ops Series
Targeted
Bound to Danger
Chasing Danger (novella)
Shattered Duty
Edge of Danger
A Covert Affair

Non-series Romantic Suspense
Running From the Past
Dangerous Secrets
Killer Secrets
Deadly Obsession
Danger in Paradise
His Secret Past
Retribution
Merry Christmas, Baby

Paranormal Romance
Destined Mate
Protector's Mate
A Jaguar's Kiss
Tempting the Jaguar
Enemy Mine
Heart of the Jaguar

Moon Shifter Series
Alpha Instinct
Lover's Instinct (novella)
Primal Possession
Mating Instinct
His Untamed Desire (novella)
Avenger's Heat
Hunter Reborn
Protective Instinct (novella)

Darkness Series
Darkness Awakened
Taste of Darkness
Beyond the Darkness
Hunted by Darkness
Into the Darkness

ABOUT THE AUTHOR

Katie Reus is the *New York Times* and *USA Today* bestselling author of the Red Stone Security series, the Darkness series and the Deadly Ops series. She fell in love with romance at a young age thanks to books she pilfered from her mom's stash. Years later she loves reading romance almost as much as she loves writing it.

However, she didn't always know she wanted to be a writer. After changing majors many times, she finally graduated summa cum laude with a degree in psychology. Not long after that she discovered a new love. Writing. She now spends her days writing dark paranormal romance and sexy romantic suspense.

For more information on Katie please visit her website: www.katiereus.com. Also find her on twitter @katiereus or visit her on facebook at: www.facebook.com/katiereusauthor.

Made in the USA
Middletown, DE
02 October 2017